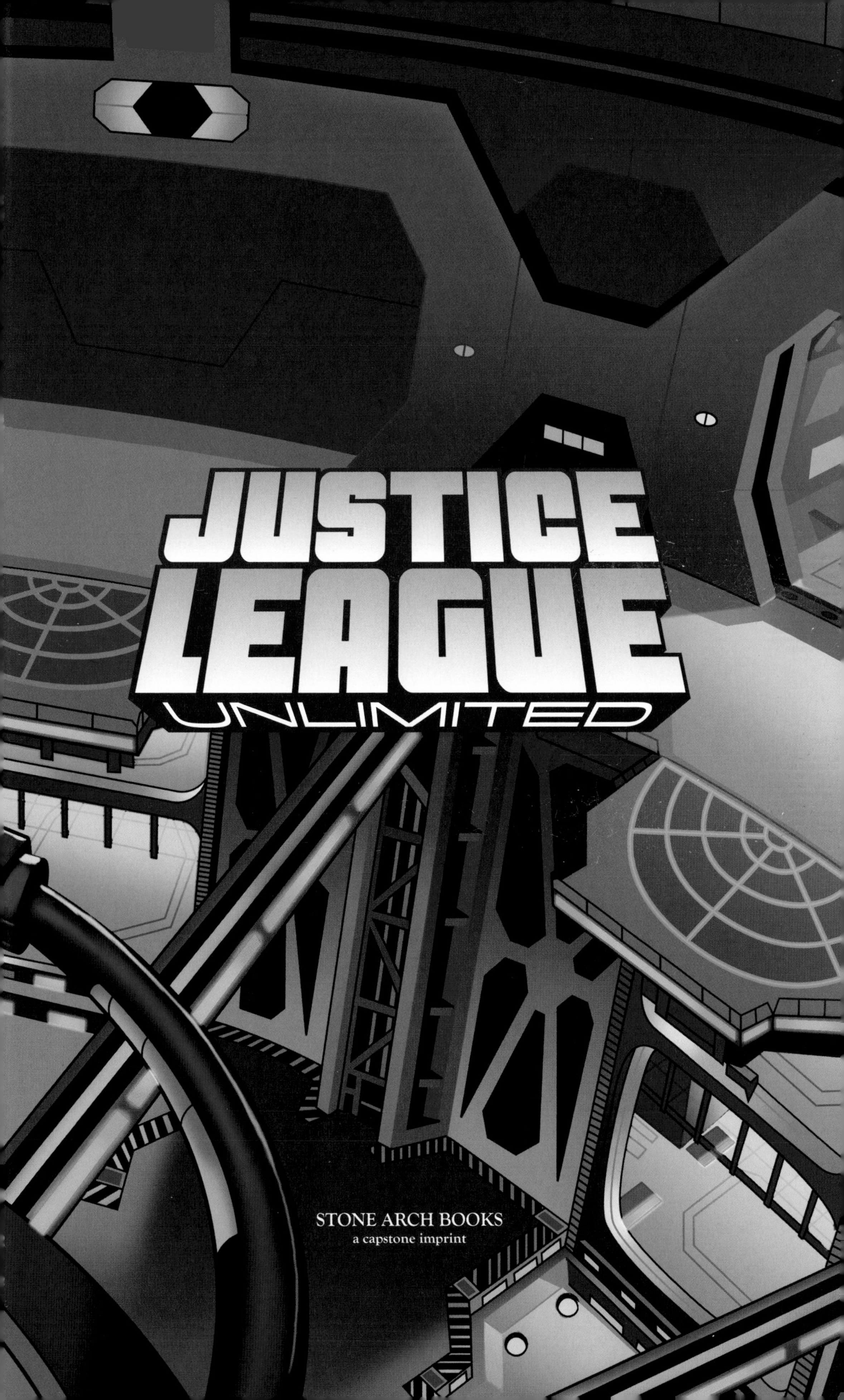

JUSTICE LEAGUE UNLIMITED

STONE ARCH BOOKS
a capstone imprint

▼▼ STONE ARCH BOOKS™

Published in 2013
A Capstone Imprint
1710 Roe Crest Drive
North Mankato, MN 56003
www.capstonepub.com

Originally published by DC Comics in the U.S. in single
magazine form as Justice League Unlimited #5.
Copyright © 2013 DC Comics. All Rights Reserved.

DC Comics
1700 Broadway, New York, NY 10019
A Warner Bros. Entertainment Company

Printed in China by Nordica.
0413/CA21300442
032013   007226NORDF13

Cataloging-in-Publication Data is available
at the Library of Congress website:
ISBN: 978-1-4342-6041-3 (library binding)

Summary: Blue Beetle is ready to enjoy
a relaxing night of monitor duty at the
Watchtower. But when chaos erupts across
the globe, Blue Beetle realizes he's the only
team member on call. Yikes!

STONE ARCH BOOKS

Ashley C. Andersen Zantop *Publisher*

Michael Dahl *Editorial Director*
Sean Tulien & Donald Lemke *Editors*
Heather Kindseth *Creative Director*
Bob Lentz & Hilary Wacholz *Designers*
Kathy McColley *Production Specialist*

DC COMICS

Tom Palmer Jr. *Original U.S. Editor*

JUSTICE LEAGUE UNLIMITED

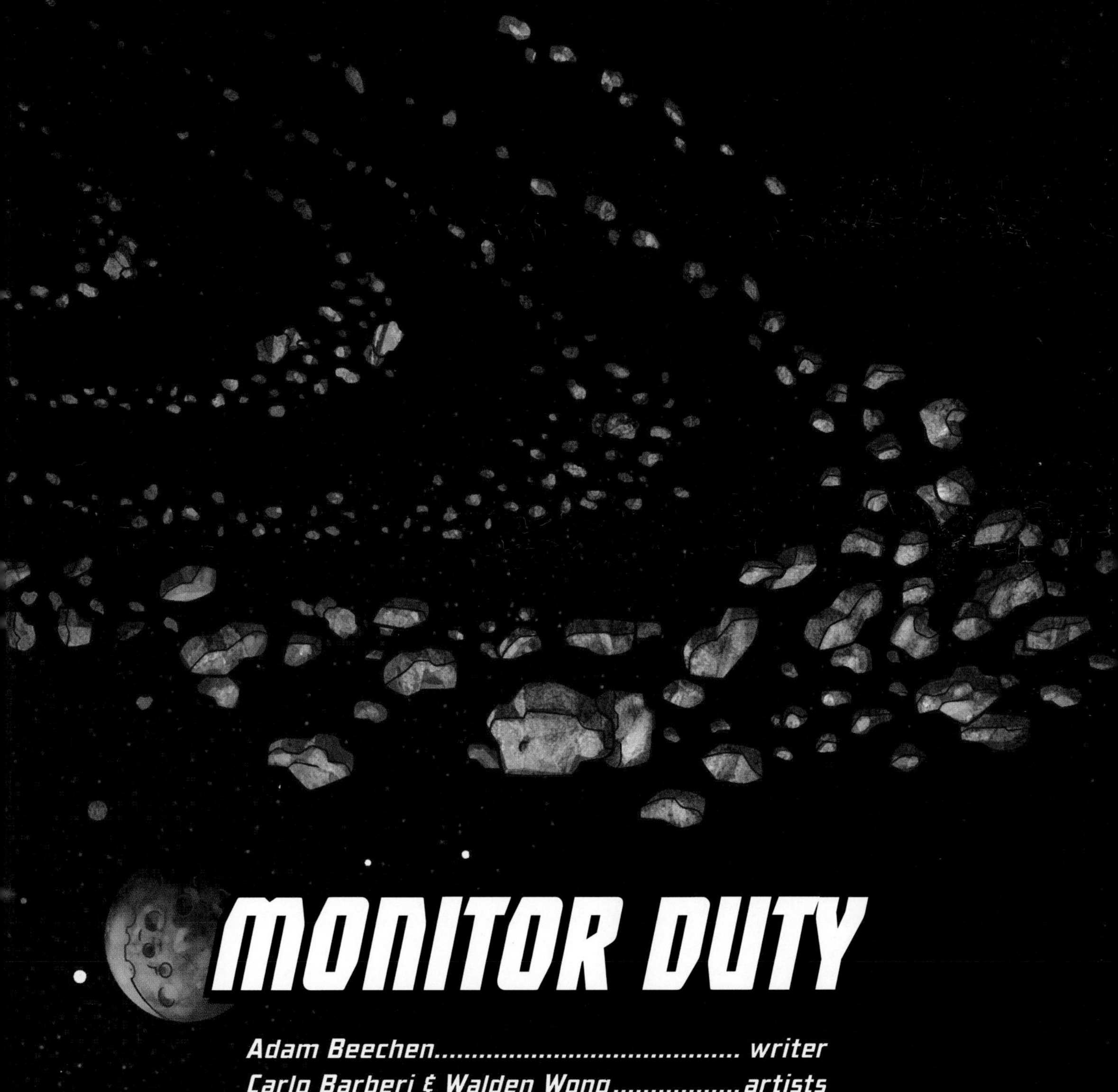

MONITOR DUTY

Adam Beechen.. writer
Carlo Barberi & Walden Wong.................artists
Heroic Age ....colorist
Phil Balsman..letterer

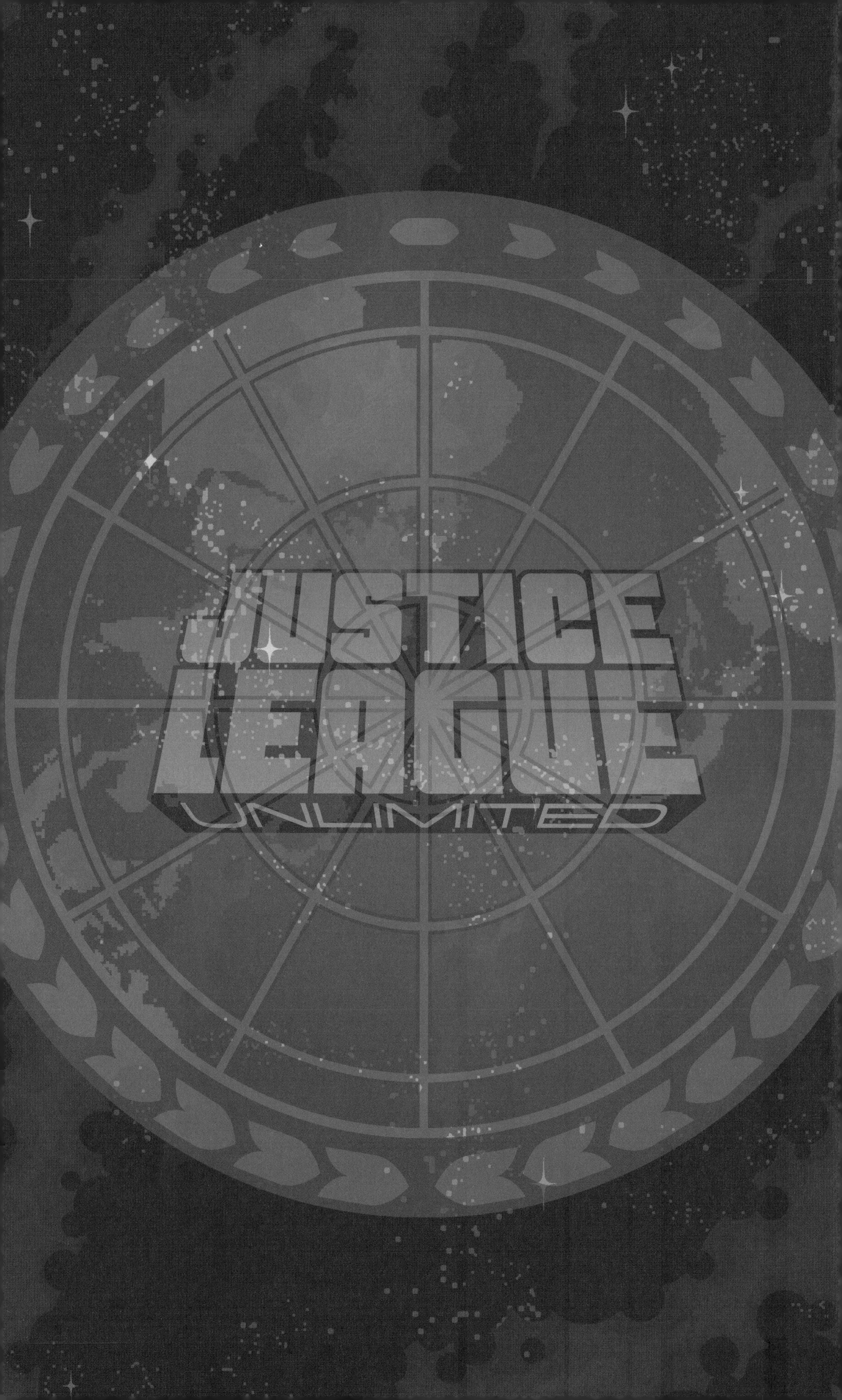
JUSTICE
LEAGUE
UNLIMITED

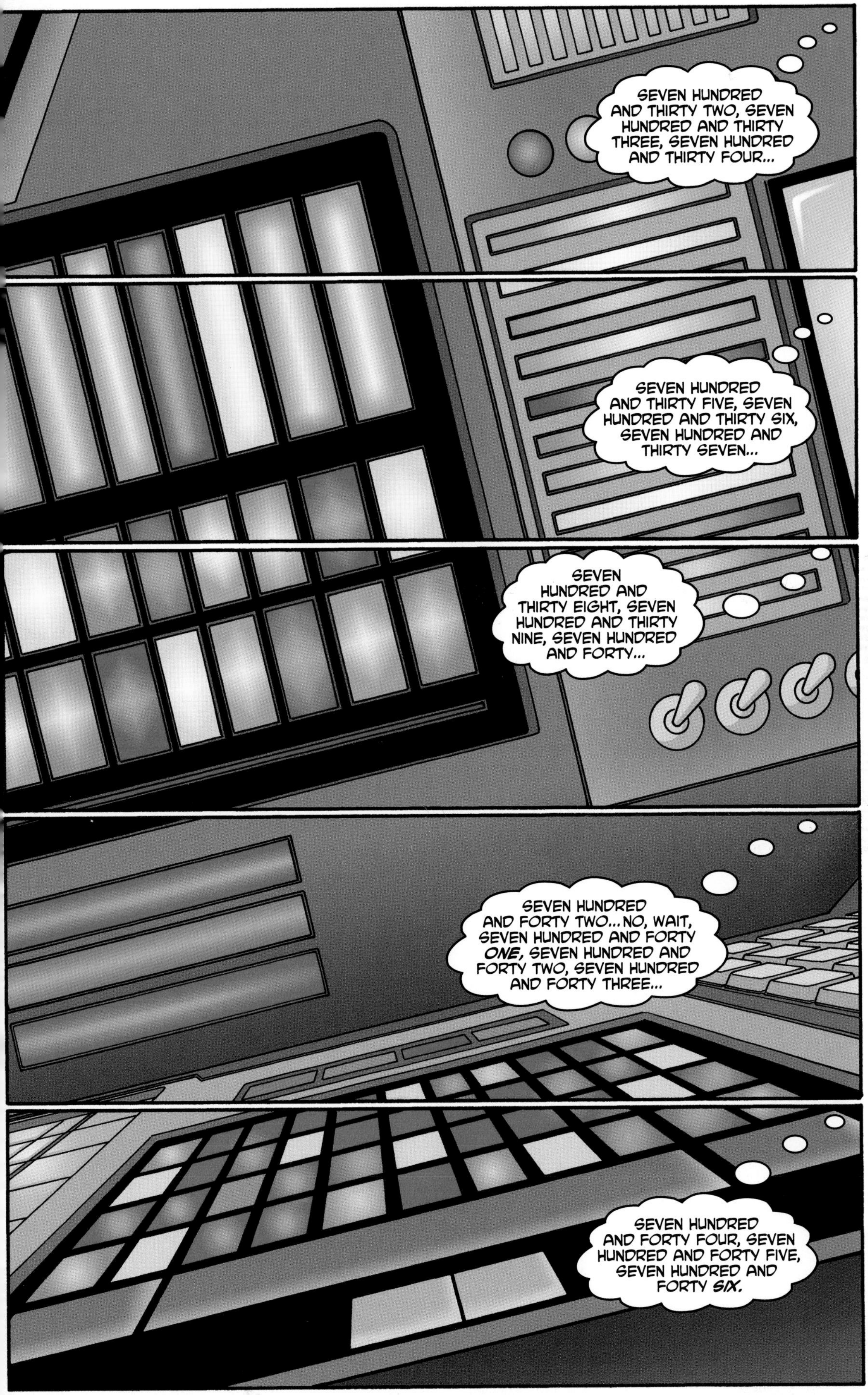
SEVEN HUNDRED AND THIRTY TWO, SEVEN HUNDRED AND THIRTY THREE, SEVEN HUNDRED AND THIRTY FOUR...
SEVEN HUNDRED AND THIRTY FIVE, SEVEN HUNDRED AND THIRTY SIX, SEVEN HUNDRED AND THIRTY SEVEN...
SEVEN HUNDRED AND THIRTY EIGHT, SEVEN HUNDRED AND THIRTY NINE, SEVEN HUNDRED AND FORTY...
SEVEN HUNDRED AND FORTY TWO... NO, WAIT, SEVEN HUNDRED AND FORTY *ONE,* SEVEN HUNDRED AND FORTY TWO, SEVEN HUNDRED AND FORTY THREE...
SEVEN HUNDRED AND FORTY FOUR, SEVEN HUNDRED AND FORTY FIVE, SEVEN HUNDRED AND FORTY *SIX.*

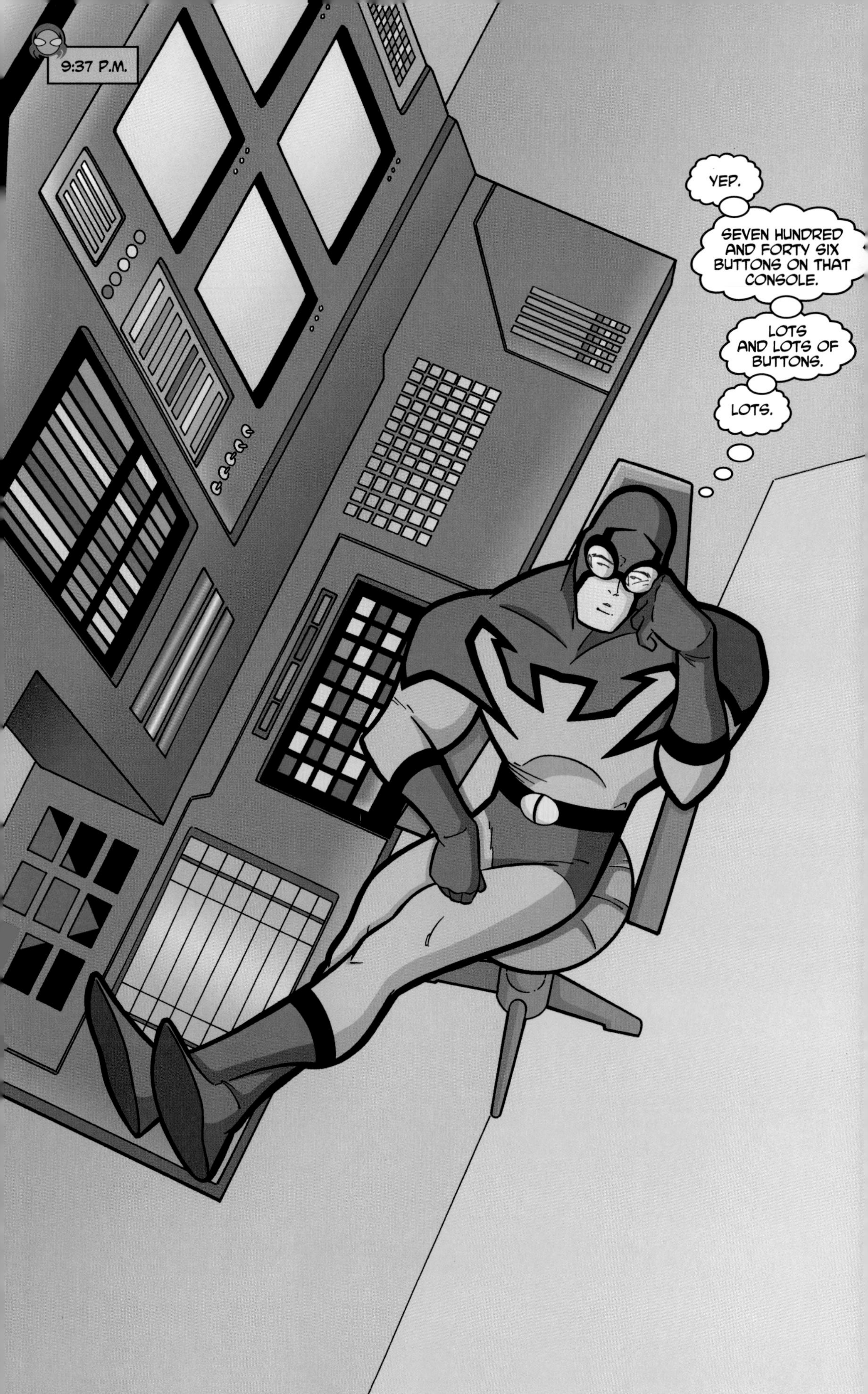

9:37 P.M.
YEP.
SEVEN HUNDRED AND FORTY SIX BUTTONS ON THAT CONSOLE.
LOTS AND LOTS OF BUTTONS.
LOTS.

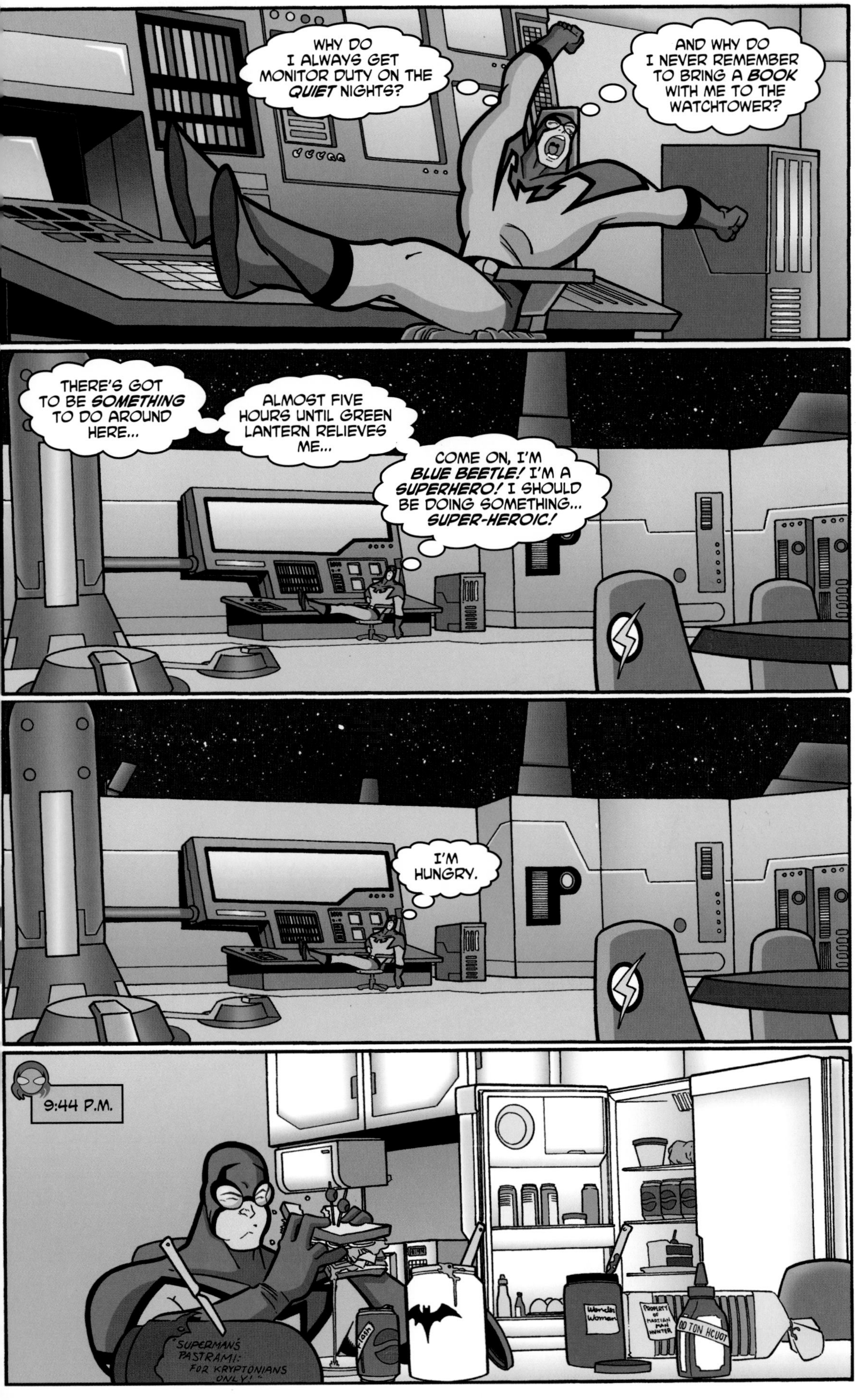
WHY DO I ALWAYS GET MONITOR DUTY ON THE *QUIET* NIGHTS?
AND WHY DO I NEVER REMEMBER TO BRING A *BOOK* WITH ME TO THE WATCHTOWER?
THERE'S GOT TO BE *SOMETHING* TO DO AROUND HERE...
ALMOST FIVE HOURS UNTIL GREEN LANTERN RELIEVES ME...
COME ON, I'M *BLUE BEETLE!* I'M A *SUPERHERO!* I SHOULD BE DOING SOMETHING... *SUPER-HEROIC!*
I'M HUNGRY.
9:44 P.M.
"SUPERMAN'S PASTRAMI: FOR KRYPTONIANS ONLY!"
Wonder Woman
PROPERTY OF MARTIAN MAN HUNTER

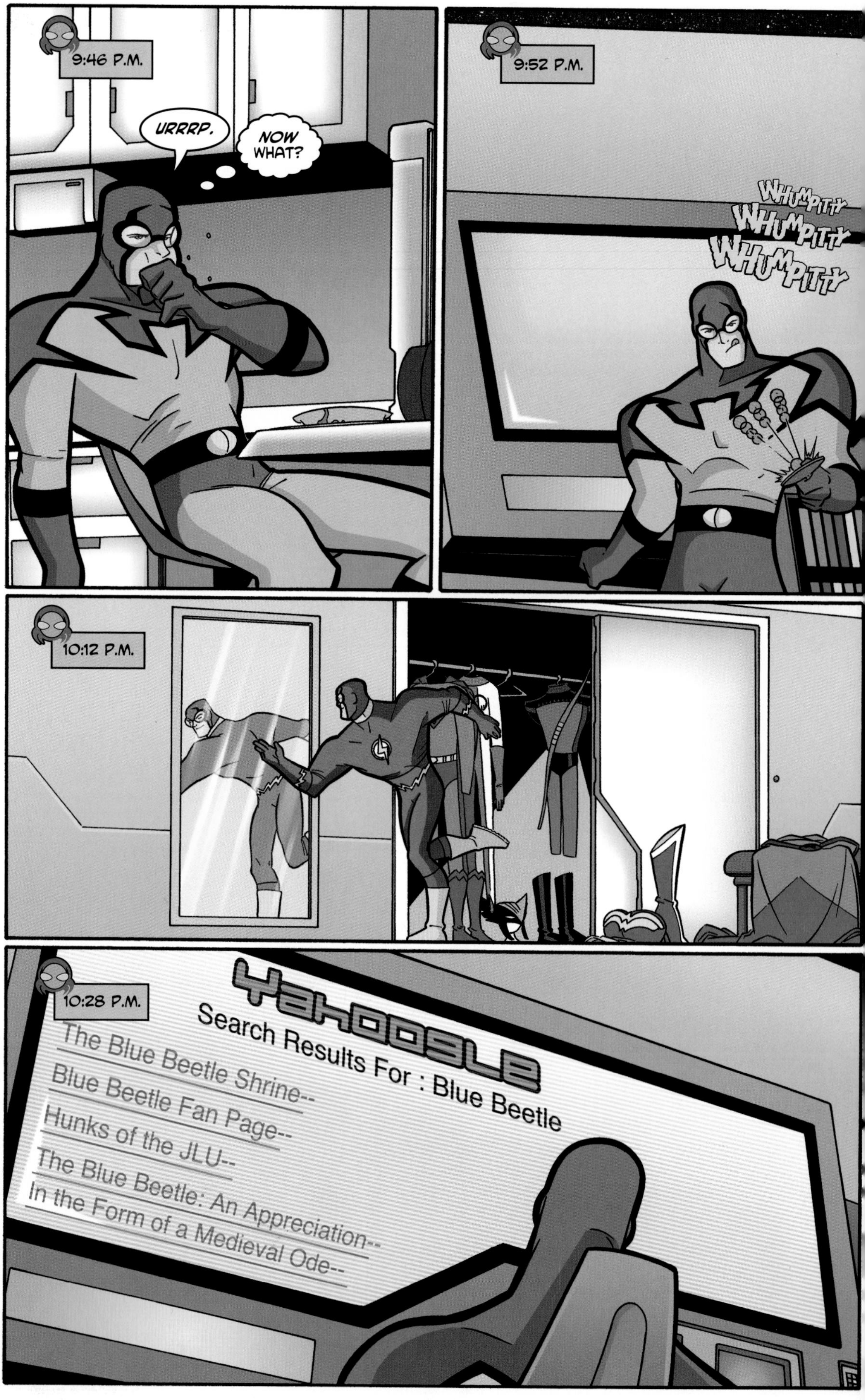

9:46 P.M.
URRRP.
NOW WHAT?
9:52 P.M.
WHUMPITTY
WHUMPITTY
WHUMPITTY
10:12 P.M.
10:28 P.M.
YAHOOGLE
Search Results For : Blue Beetle
The Blue Beetle Shrine--
Blue Beetle Fan Page--
Hunks of the JLU--
The Blue Beetle: An Appreciation--
In the Form of a Medieval Ode--

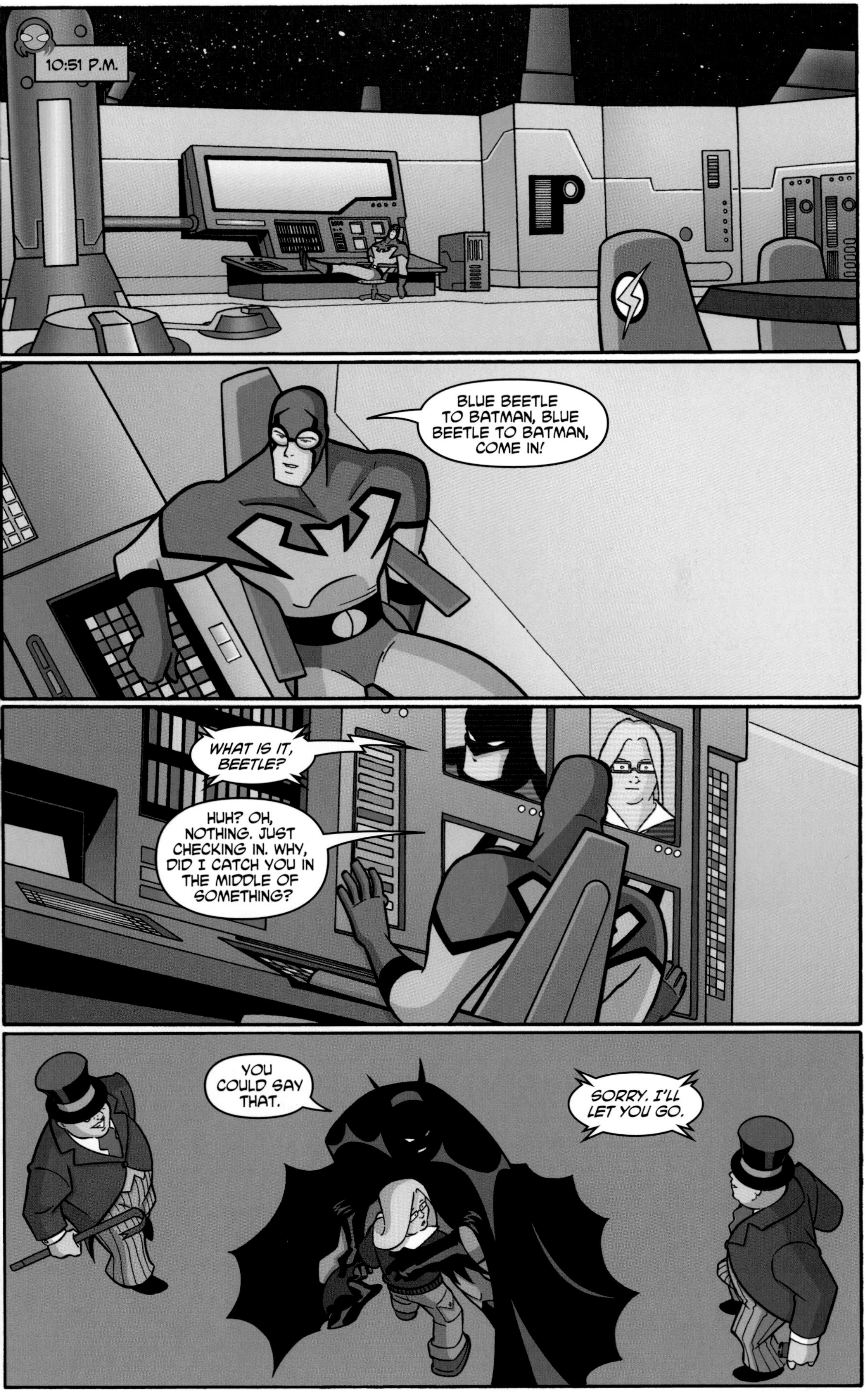
10:51 P.M.
BLUE BEETLE TO BATMAN, BLUE BEETLE TO BATMAN, COME IN!
WHAT IS IT, BEETLE?
HUH? OH, NOTHING. JUST CHECKING IN. WHY, DID I CATCH YOU IN THE MIDDLE OF SOMETHING?
YOU COULD SAY THAT.
SORRY. I'LL LET YOU GO.

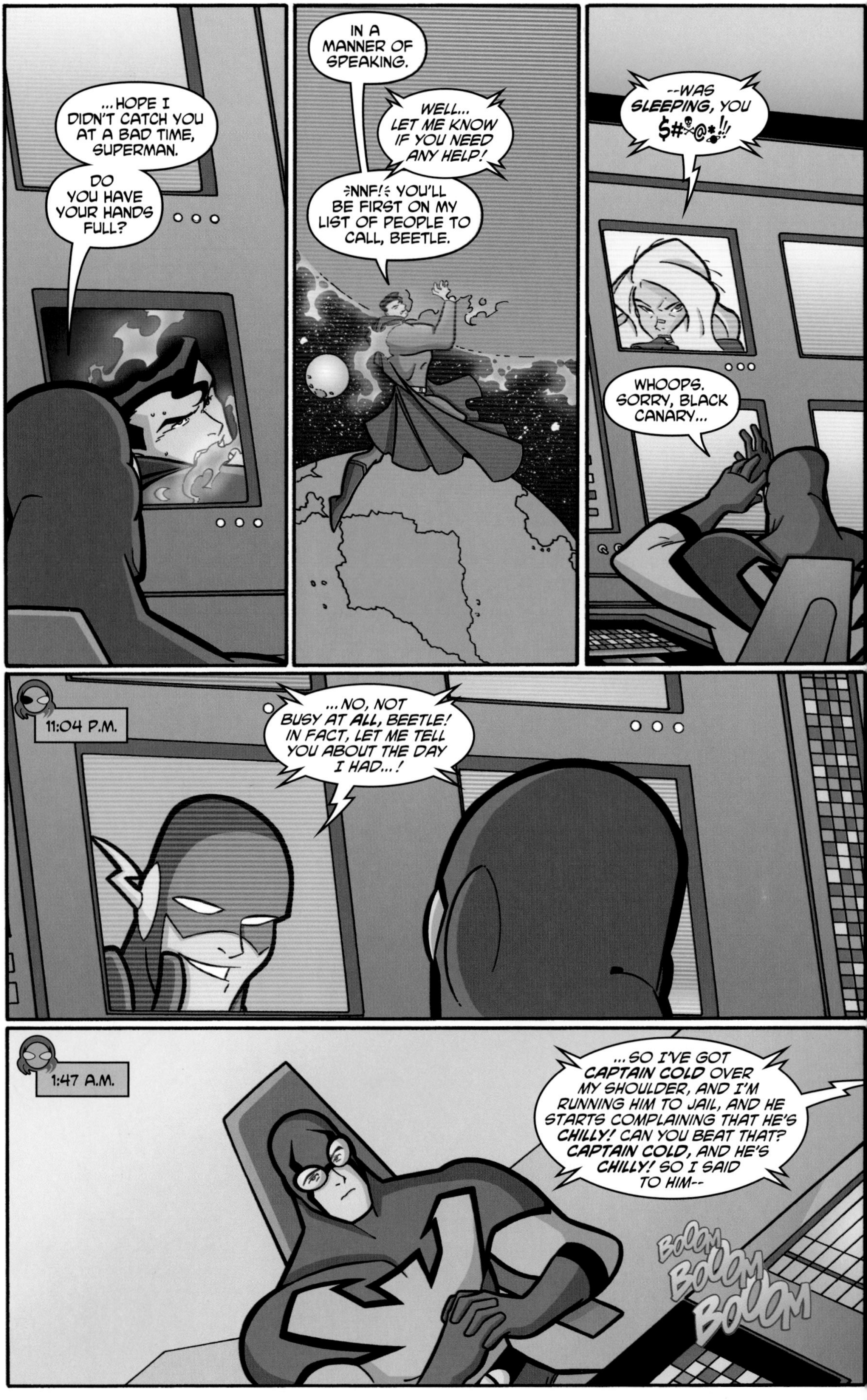
...HOPE I DIDN'T CATCH YOU AT A BAD TIME, SUPERMAN.
DO YOU HAVE YOUR HANDS FULL?
IN A MANNER OF SPEAKING.
WELL... LET ME KNOW IF YOU NEED ANY HELP!
NNF! YOU'LL BE FIRST ON MY LIST OF PEOPLE TO CALL, BEETLE.
--WAS SLEEPING, YOU $#☠@*!!
WHOOPS. SORRY, BLACK CANARY...
11:04 P.M.
...NO, NOT BUSY AT ALL, BEETLE! IN FACT, LET ME TELL YOU ABOUT THE DAY I HAD...!
1:47 A.M.
...SO I'VE GOT CAPTAIN COLD OVER MY SHOULDER, AND I'M RUNNING HIM TO JAIL, AND HE STARTS COMPLAINING THAT HE'S CHILLY! CAN YOU BEAT THAT? CAPTAIN COLD, AND HE'S CHILLY! SO I SAID TO HIM--
BOOM BOOM BOOM

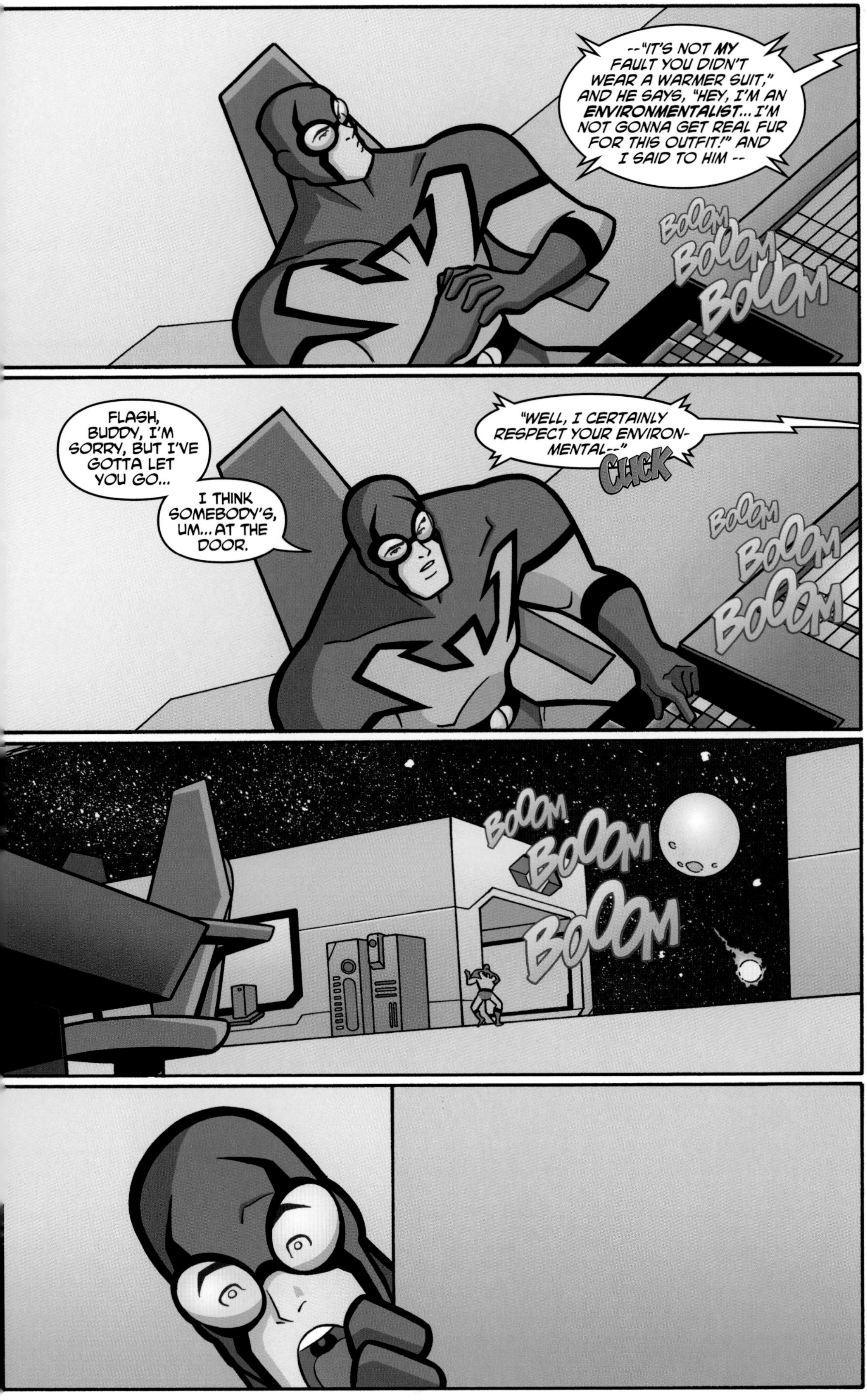
--"IT'S NOT MY FAULT YOU DIDN'T WEAR A WARMER SUIT," AND HE SAYS, "HEY, I'M AN ENVIRONMENTALIST... I'M NOT GONNA GET REAL FUR FOR THIS OUTFIT!" AND I SAID TO HIM --
BOOOM BOOOM BOOOM
"WELL, I CERTAINLY RESPECT YOUR ENVIRON-MENTAL--"
CLICK
FLASH, BUDDY, I'M SORRY, BUT I'VE GOTTA LET YOU GO...
I THINK SOMEBODY'S, UM... AT THE DOOR.
BOOOM BOOOM BOOOM
BOOOM BOOOM BOOOM

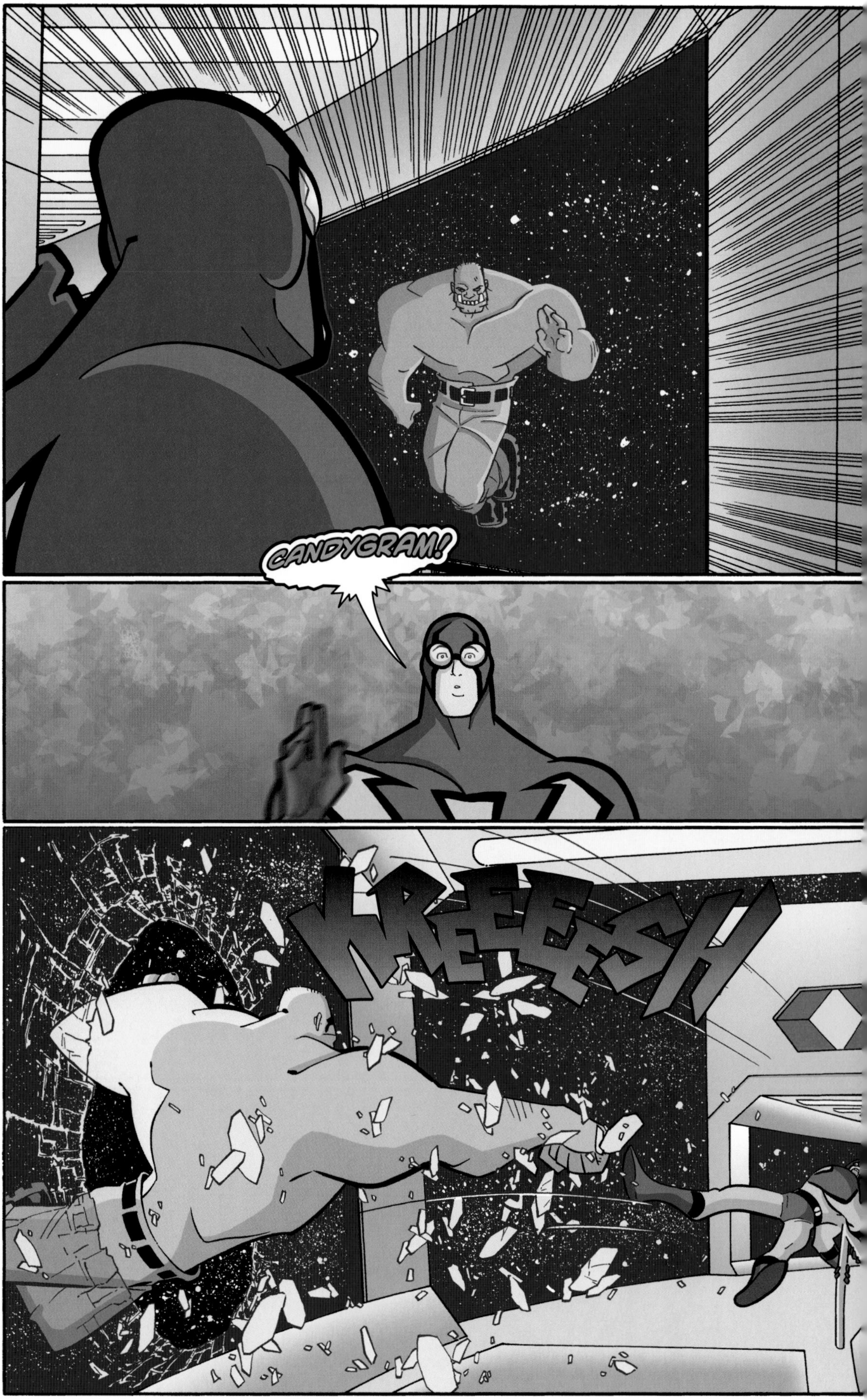
CANDYGRAM!
KREEESH

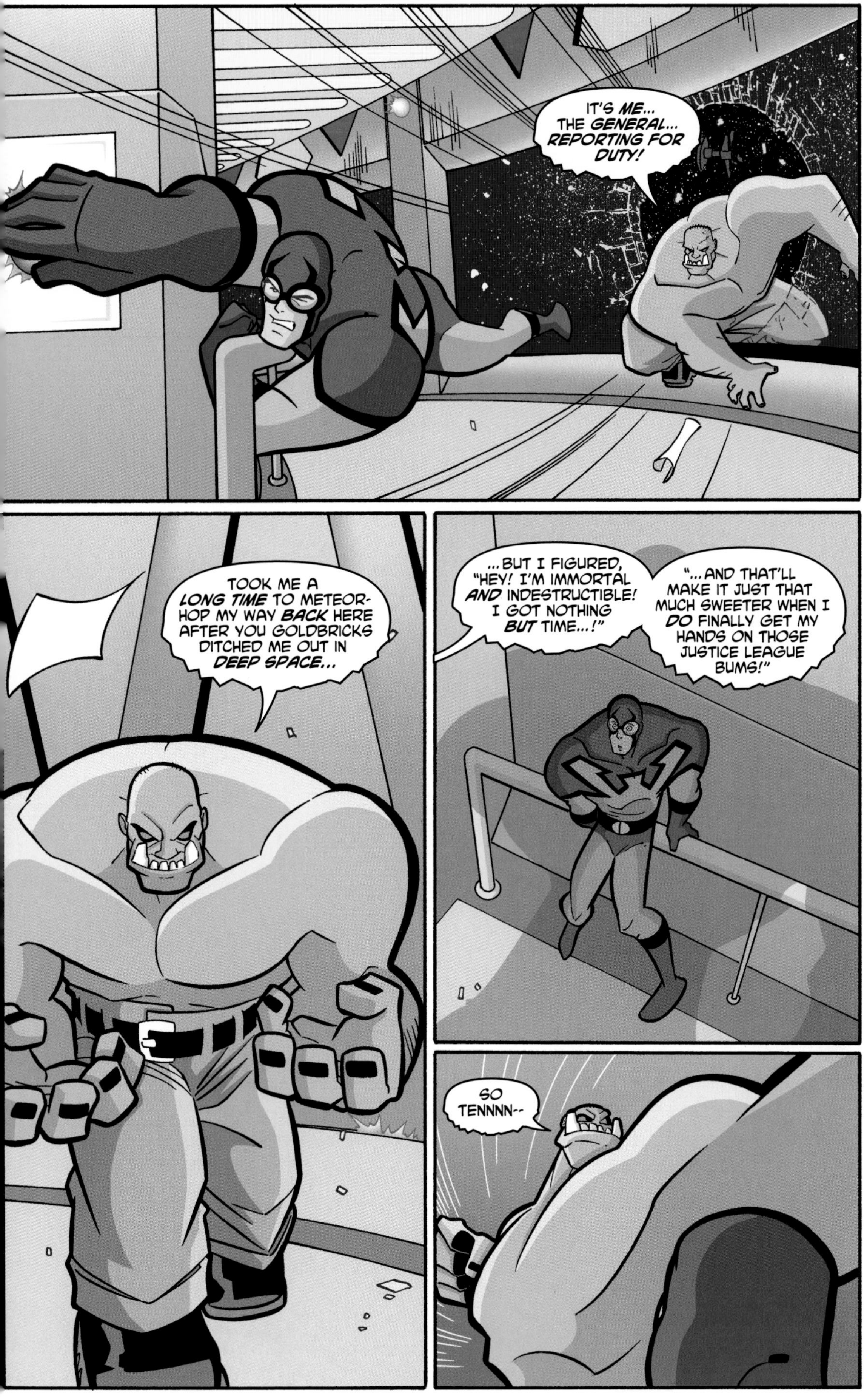

IT'S ME... THE GENERAL... REPORTING FOR DUTY!
TOOK ME A LONG TIME TO METEOR-HOP MY WAY BACK HERE AFTER YOU GOLDBRICKS DITCHED ME OUT IN DEEP SPACE...
...BUT I FIGURED, "HEY! I'M IMMORTAL AND INDESTRUCTIBLE! I GOT NOTHING BUT TIME...!"
"...AND THAT'LL MAKE IT JUST THAT MUCH SWEETER WHEN I DO FINALLY GET MY HANDS ON THOSE JUSTICE LEAGUE BUMS!"
SO TENNNN--

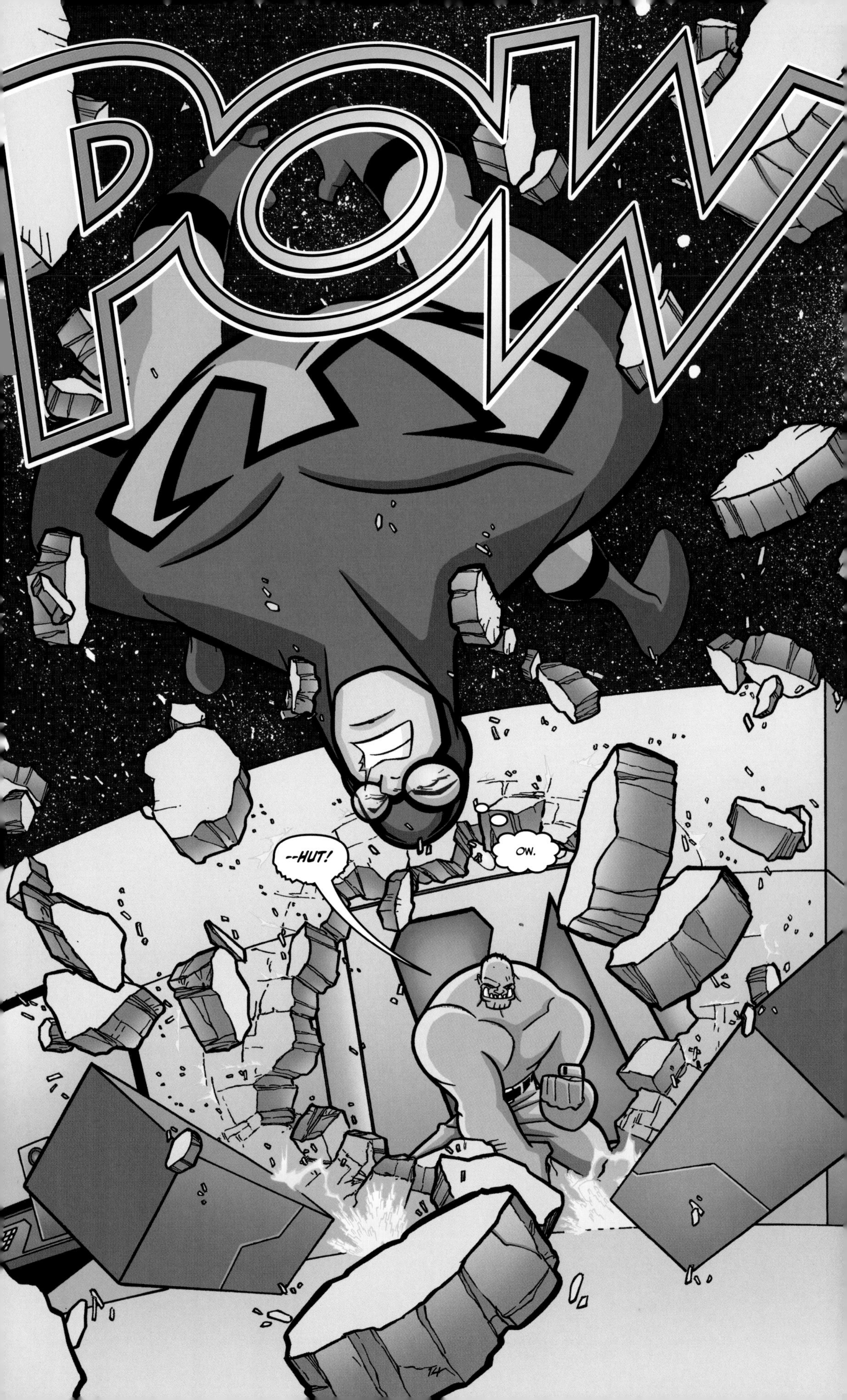
POW
--HUT!
OW.

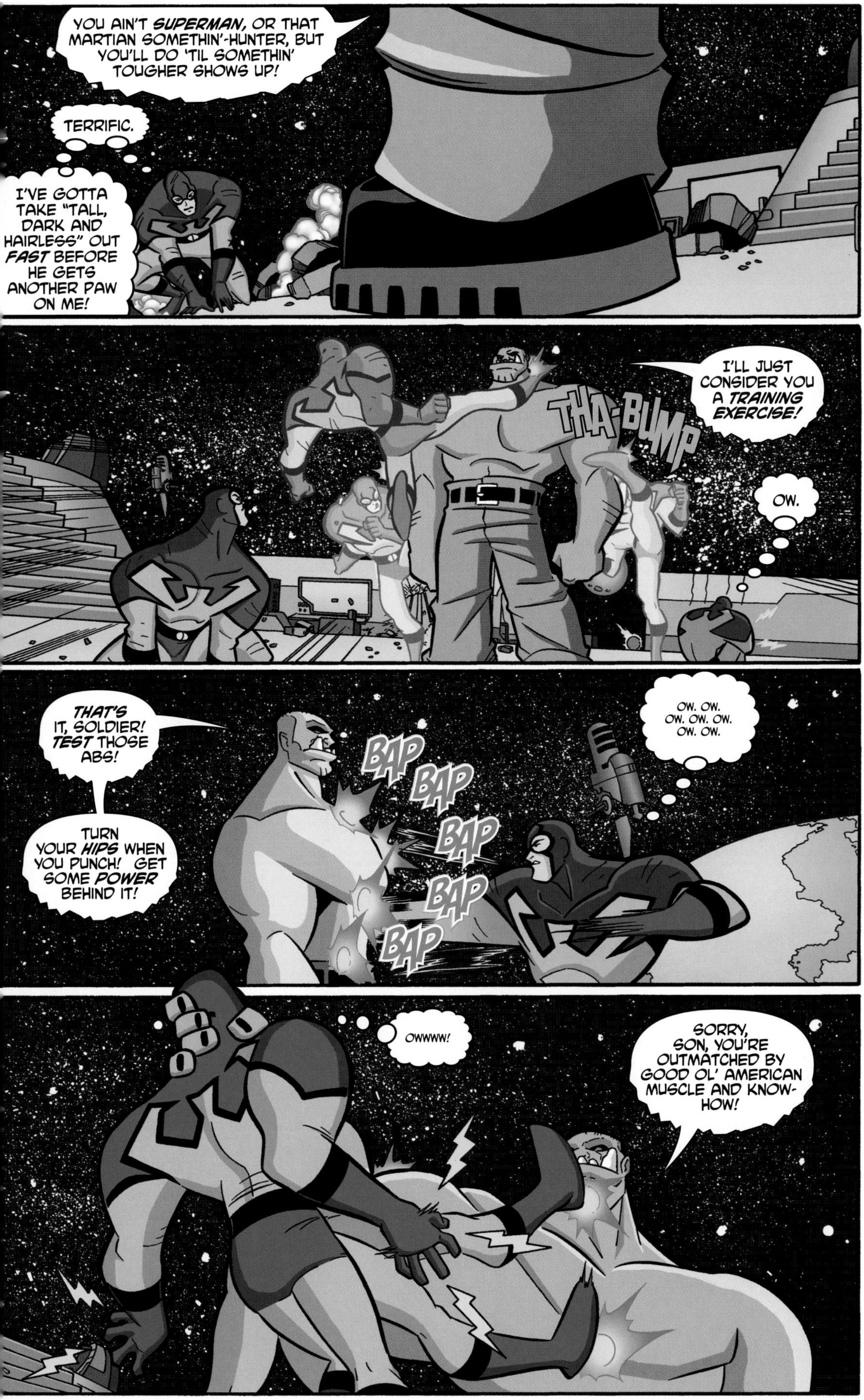
YOU AIN'T SUPERMAN, OR THAT MARTIAN SOMETHIN'-HUNTER, BUT YOU'LL DO 'TIL SOMETHIN' TOUGHER SHOWS UP!
TERRIFIC.
I'VE GOTTA TAKE "TALL, DARK AND HAIRLESS" OUT FAST BEFORE HE GETS ANOTHER PAW ON ME!
THA-BUMP
I'LL JUST CONSIDER YOU A TRAINING EXERCISE!
OW.
THAT'S IT, SOLDIER! TEST THOSE ABS!
TURN YOUR HIPS WHEN YOU PUNCH! GET SOME POWER BEHIND IT!
BAP BAP BAP BAP BAP
OW. OW. OW. OW. OW. OW. OW.
OWWWW!
SORRY, SON, YOU'RE OUTMATCHED BY GOOD OL' AMERICAN MUSCLE AND KNOW-HOW!

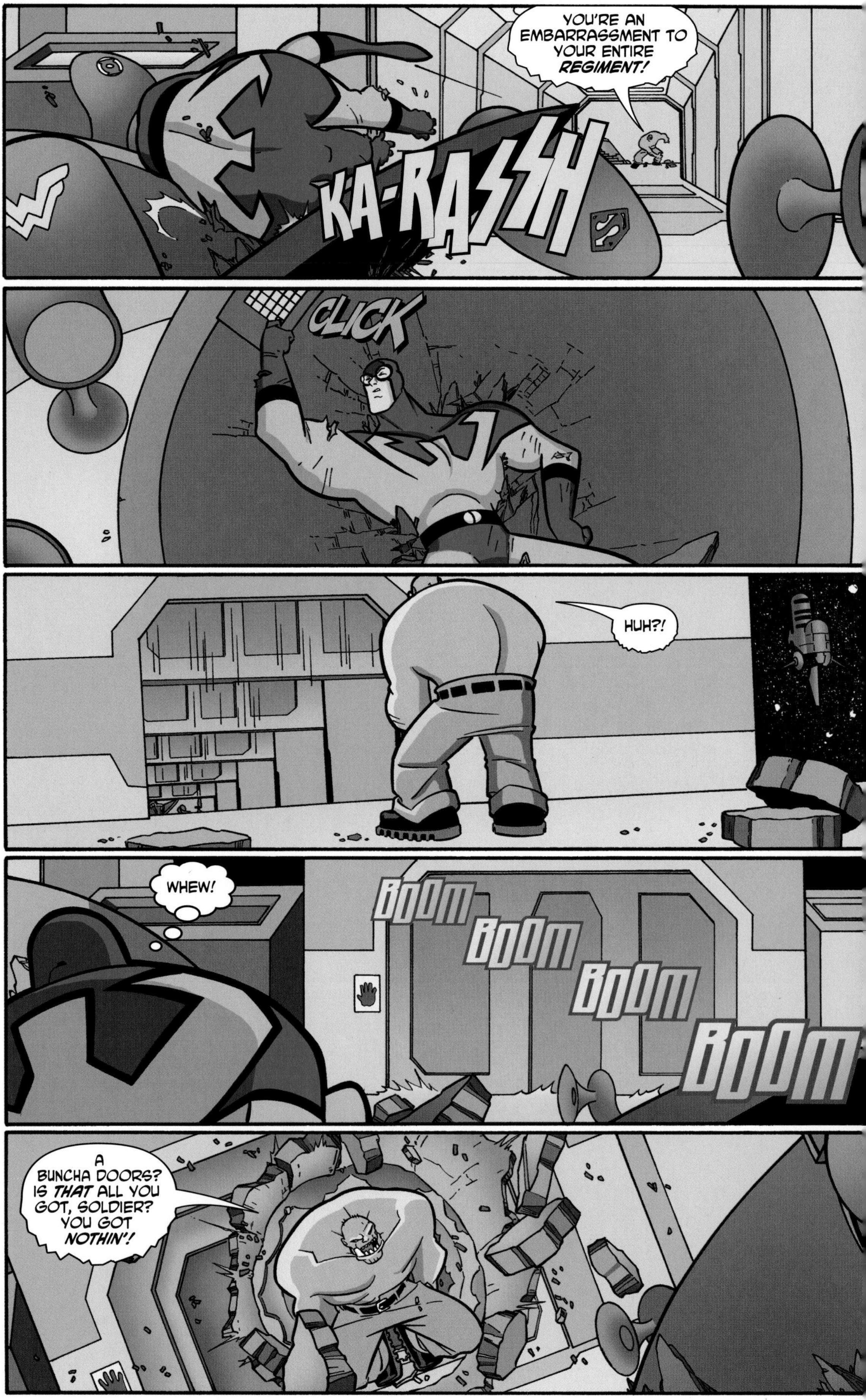
YOU'RE AN EMBARRASSMENT TO YOUR ENTIRE *REGIMENT!*
KA-RASSH
CLICK
HUH?!
WHEW!
BOOM BOOM BOOM BOOM
A BUNCHA DOORS? IS *THAT* ALL YOU GOT, SOLDIER? YOU GOT *NOTHIN'!*

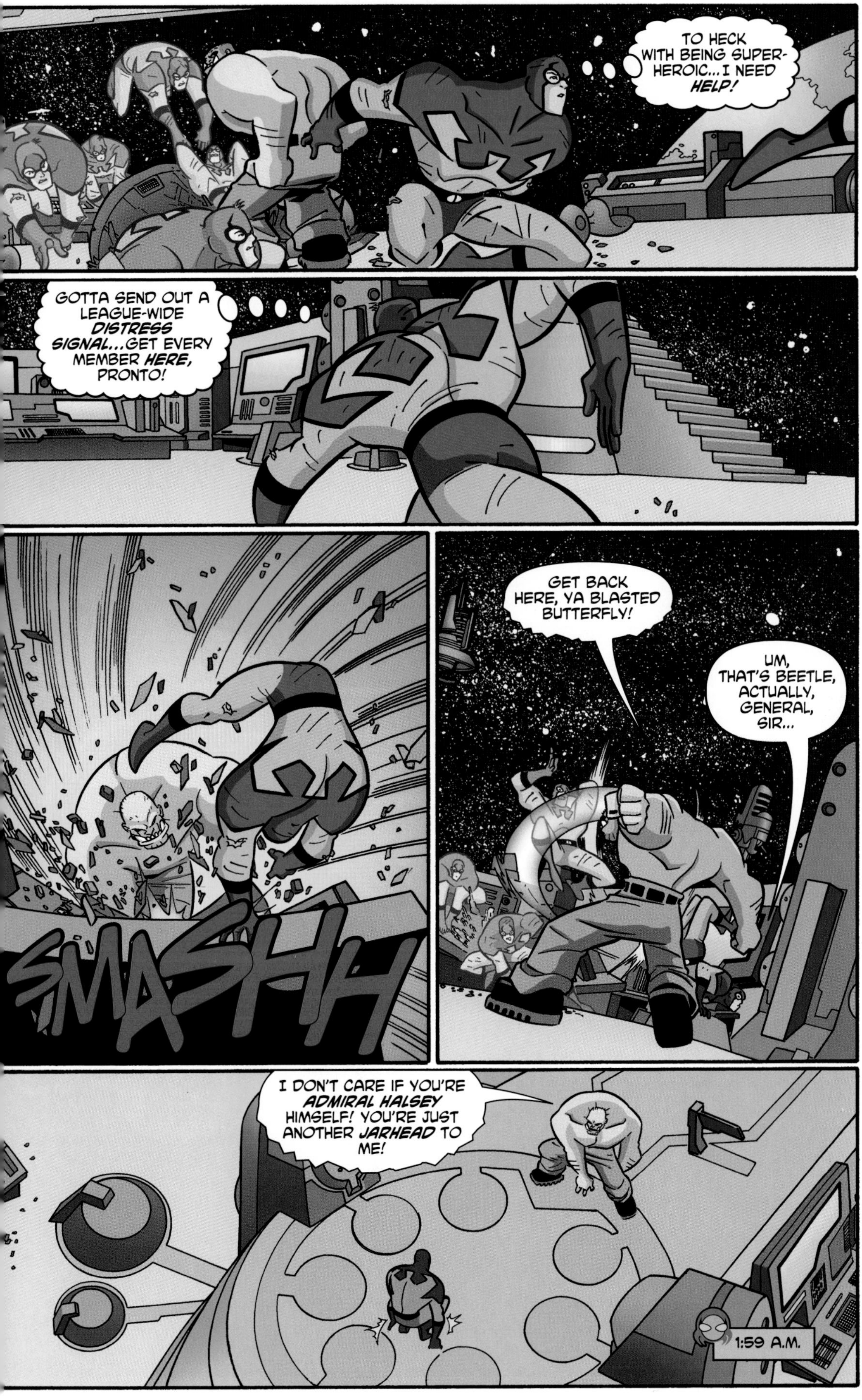

TO HECK WITH BEING SUPER-HEROIC...I NEED HELP!
GOTTA SEND OUT A LEAGUE-WIDE DISTRESS SIGNAL...GET EVERY MEMBER HERE, PRONTO!
SMASHH
GET BACK HERE, YA BLASTED BUTTERFLY!
UM, THAT'S BEETLE, ACTUALLY, GENERAL, SIR...
I DON'T CARE IF YOU'RE ADMIRAL HALSEY HIMSELF! YOU'RE JUST ANOTHER JARHEAD TO ME!
1:59 A.M.

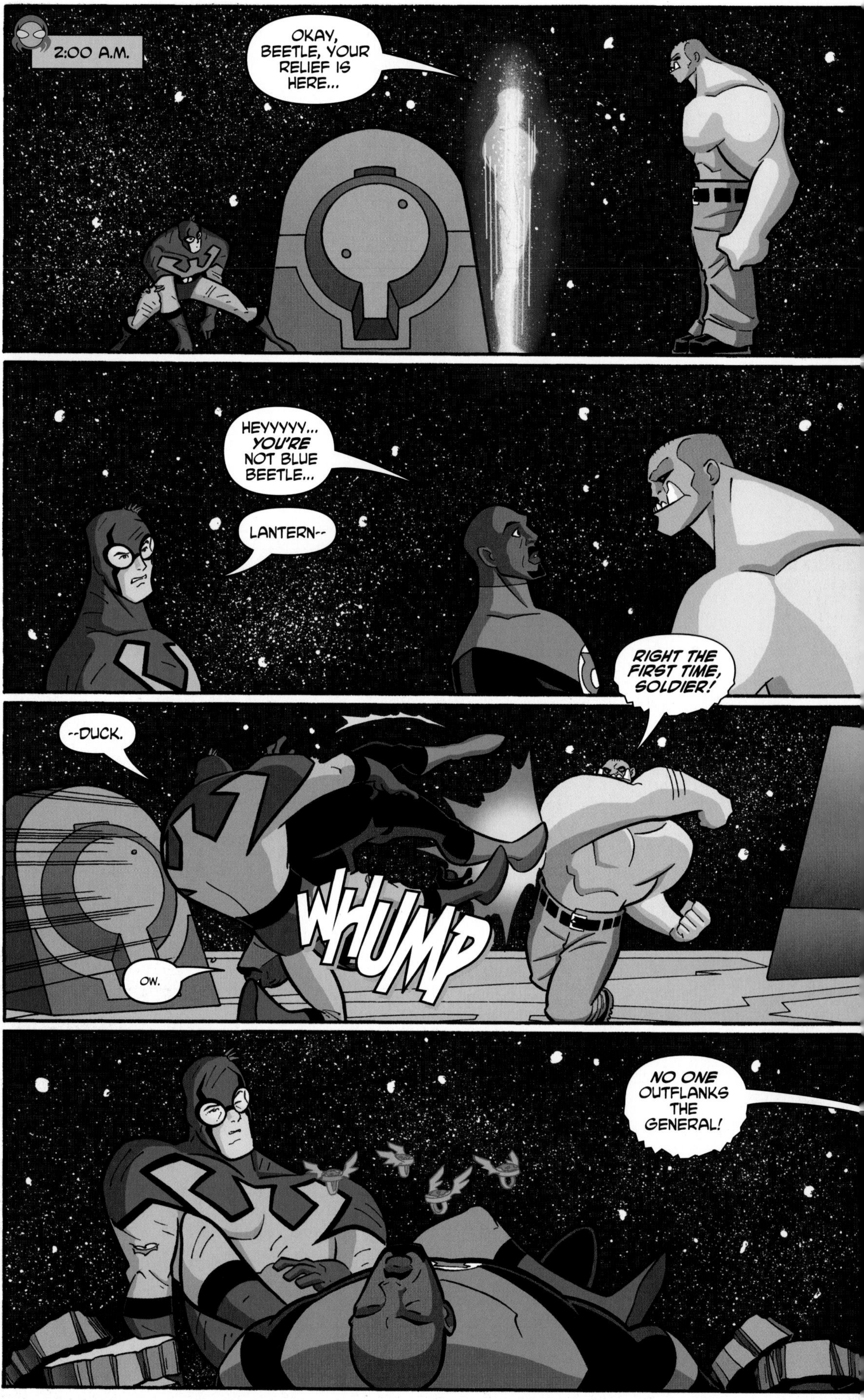

2:00 A.M.
OKAY, BEETLE, YOUR RELIEF IS HERE...
HEYYYYY... *YOU'RE* NOT BLUE BEETLE...
LANTERN--
RIGHT THE FIRST TIME, SOLDIER!
--DUCK.
WHUMP
OW.
NO ONE OUTFLANKS THE GENERAL!

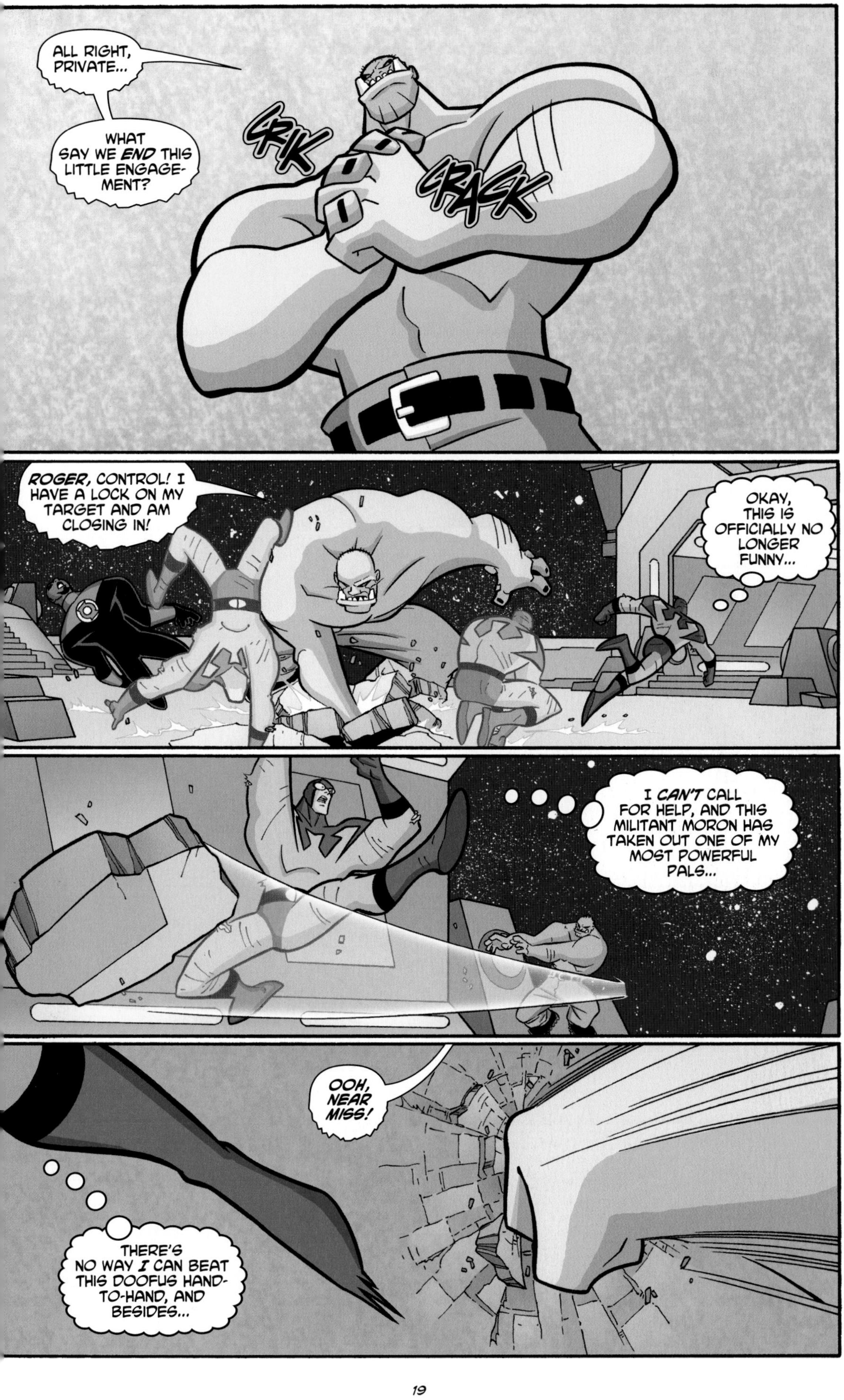
ALL RIGHT, PRIVATE...
WHAT SAY WE *END* THIS LITTLE ENGAGE-MENT?
CRIK
CRACK
ROGER, CONTROL! I HAVE A LOCK ON MY TARGET AND AM CLOSING IN!
OKAY, THIS IS OFFICIALLY NO LONGER FUNNY...
I *CAN'T* CALL FOR HELP, AND THIS MILITANT MORON HAS TAKEN OUT ONE OF MY MOST POWERFUL PALS...
OOH, NEAR MISS!
THERE'S NO WAY *I* CAN BEAT THIS DOOFUS HAND-TO-HAND, AND BESIDES...

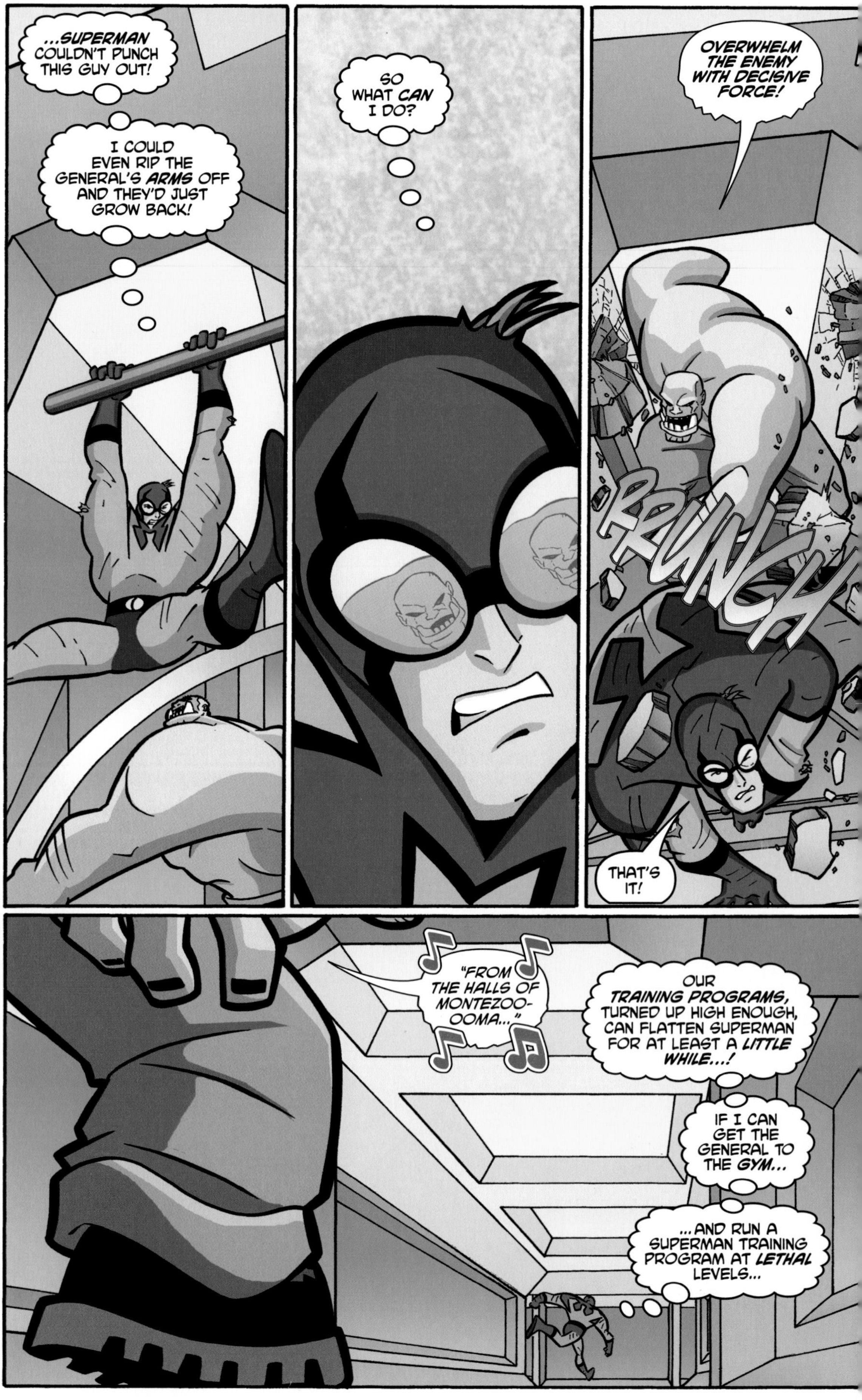
...SUPERMAN COULDN'T PUNCH THIS GUY OUT!
I COULD EVEN RIP THE GENERAL'S ARMS OFF AND THEY'D JUST GROW BACK!
SO WHAT CAN I DO?
OVERWHELM THE ENEMY WITH DECISIVE FORCE!
KRUNCH
THAT'S IT!
"FROM THE HALLS OF MONTEZOO-OOMA..."
OUR TRAINING PROGRAMS, TURNED UP HIGH ENOUGH, CAN FLATTEN SUPERMAN FOR AT LEAST A LITTLE WHILE...!
IF I CAN GET THE GENERAL TO THE GYM...
...AND RUN A SUPERMAN TRAINING PROGRAM AT LETHAL LEVELS...

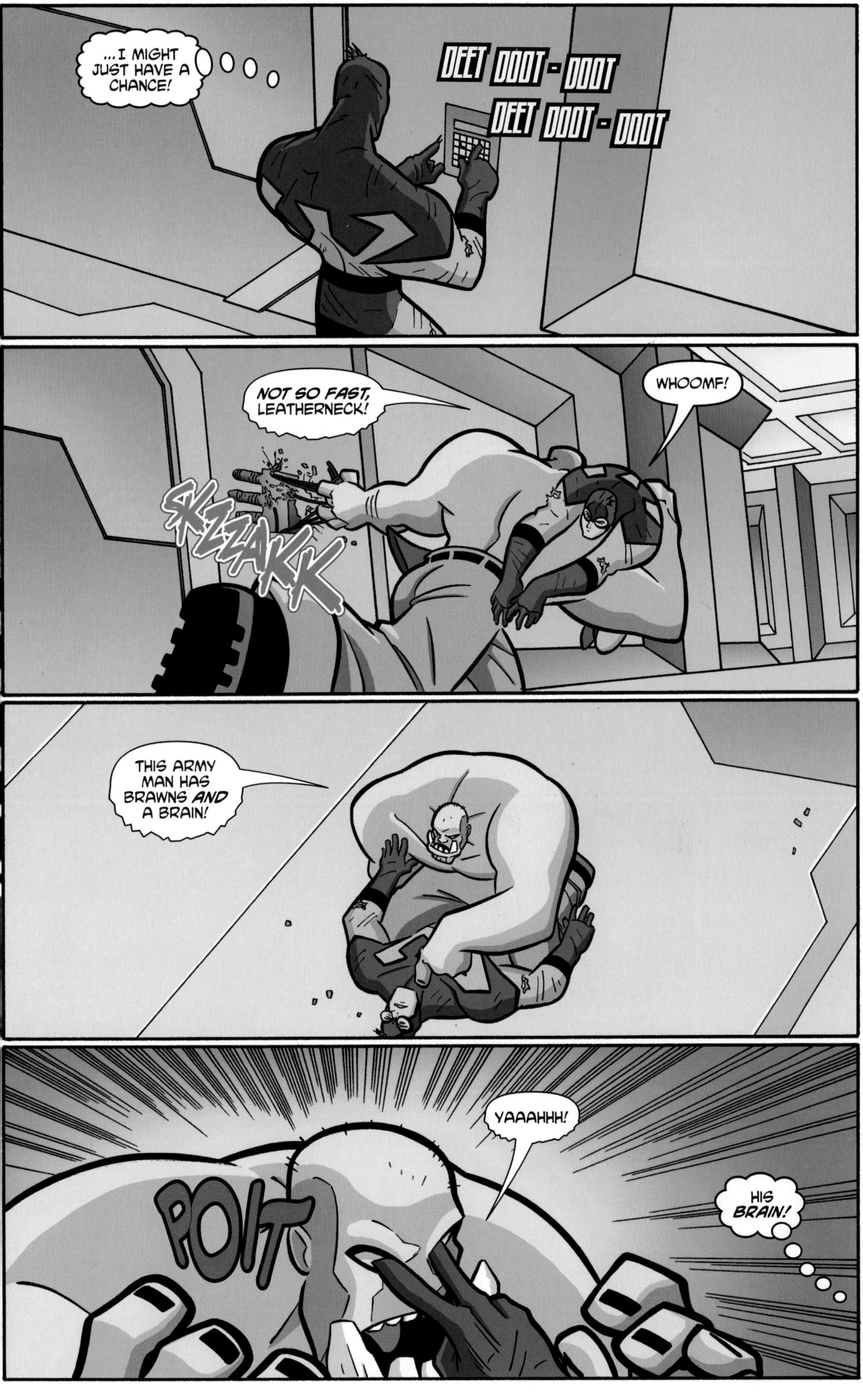
...I MIGHT JUST HAVE A CHANCE!
DEET DOOT-DOOT
DEET DOOT-DOOT
NOT SO FAST, LEATHERNECK!
WHOOMF!
SKZZZAKK
THIS ARMY MAN HAS BRAWNS AND A BRAIN!
YAAAHHH!
POIT
HIS BRAIN!

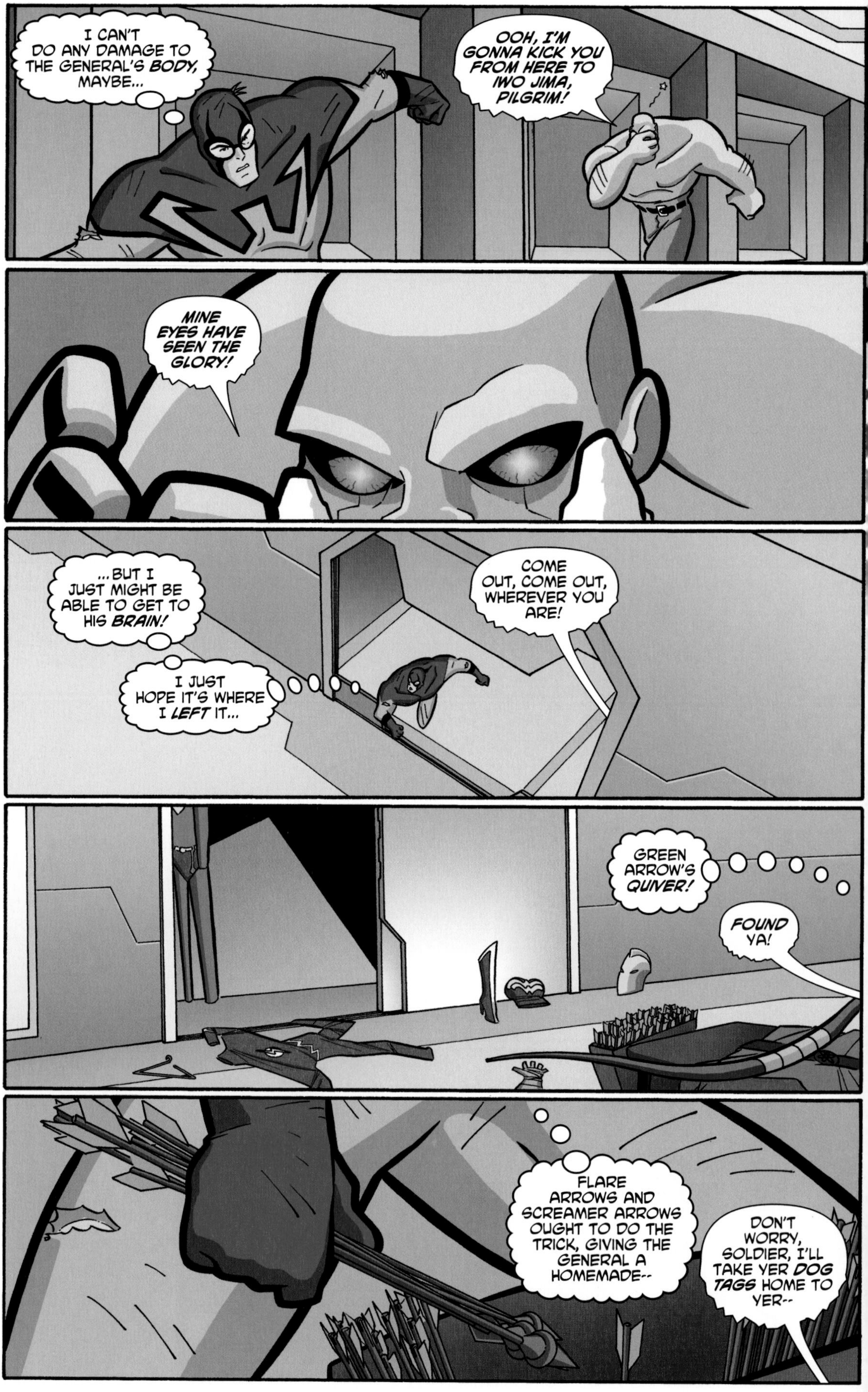
I CAN'T DO ANY DAMAGE TO THE GENERAL'S *BODY*, MAYBE...
OOH, I'M GONNA KICK YOU FROM HERE TO IWO JIMA, PILGRIM!
MINE EYES HAVE SEEN THE GLORY!
...BUT I JUST MIGHT BE ABLE TO GET TO HIS *BRAIN!*
I JUST HOPE IT'S WHERE I *LEFT* IT...
COME OUT, COME OUT, WHEREVER YOU ARE!
GREEN ARROW'S *QUIVER!*
FOUND YA!
FLARE ARROWS AND SCREAMER ARROWS OUGHT TO DO THE TRICK, GIVING THE GENERAL A HOMEMADE--
DON'T WORRY, SOLDIER, I'LL TAKE YER *DOG TAGS* HOME TO YER--

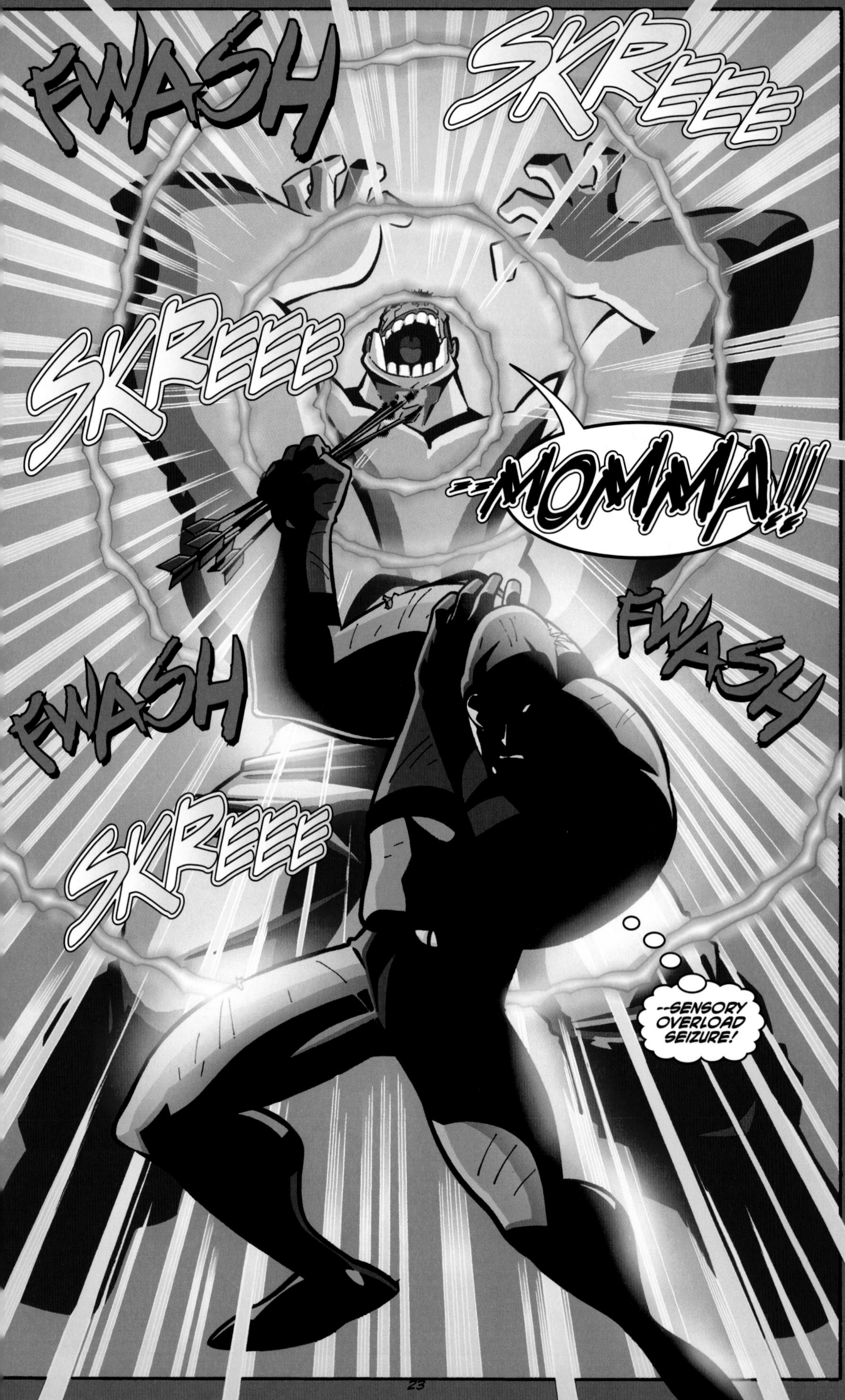
FWASH
SKREEE
SKREEE
--MOMMA!!
FWASH
FWASH
SKREEE
--SENSORY OVERLOAD SEIZURE!

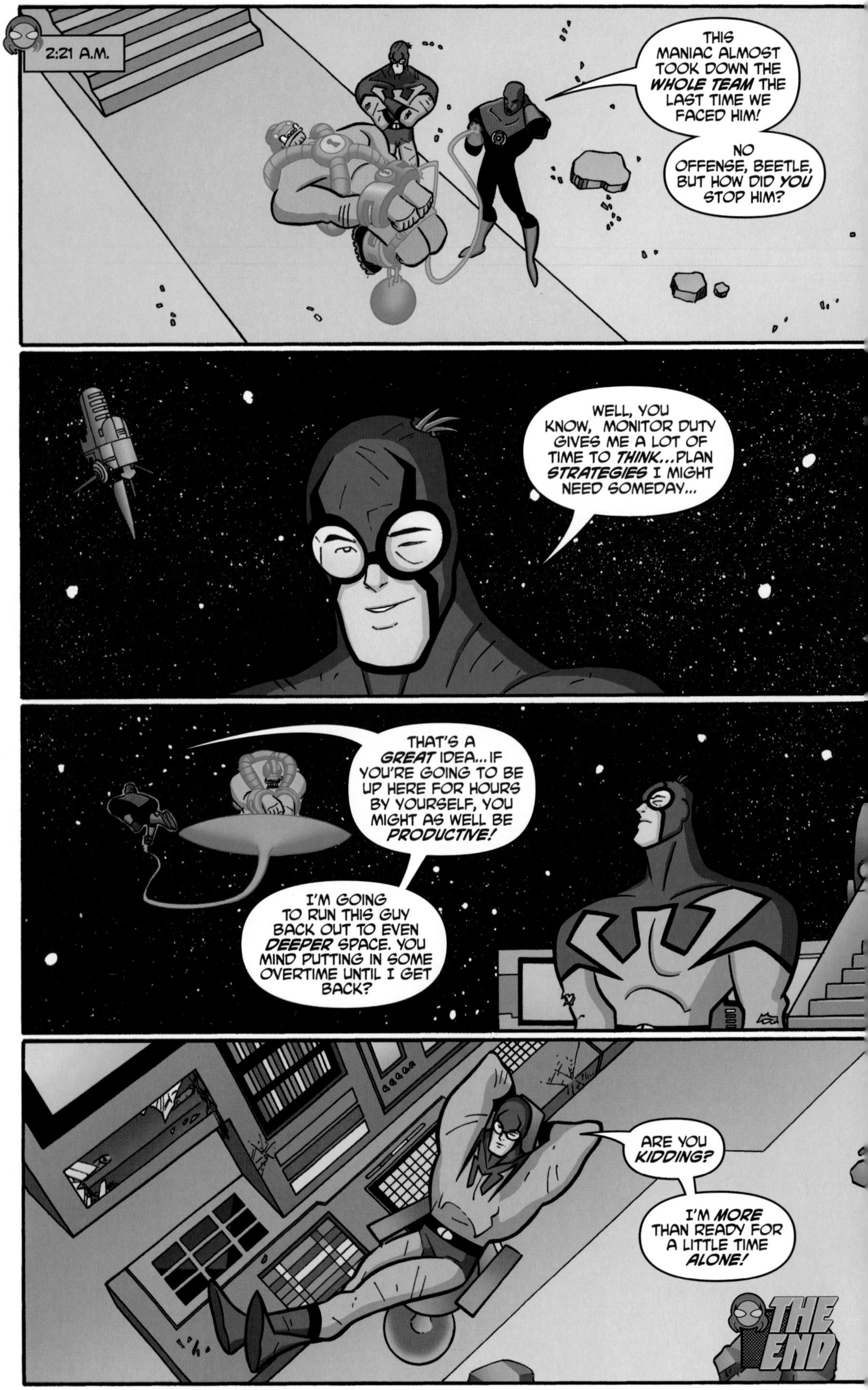
2:21 A.M.
THIS MANIAC ALMOST TOOK DOWN THE WHOLE TEAM THE LAST TIME WE FACED HIM!
NO OFFENSE, BEETLE, BUT HOW DID YOU STOP HIM?
WELL, YOU KNOW, MONITOR DUTY GIVES ME A LOT OF TIME TO THINK...PLAN STRATEGIES I MIGHT NEED SOMEDAY...
THAT'S A GREAT IDEA...IF YOU'RE GOING TO BE UP HERE FOR HOURS BY YOURSELF, YOU MIGHT AS WELL BE PRODUCTIVE!
I'M GOING TO RUN THIS GUY BACK OUT TO EVEN DEEPER SPACE. YOU MIND PUTTING IN SOME OVERTIME UNTIL I GET BACK?
ARE YOU KIDDING?
I'M MORE THAN READY FOR A LITTLE TIME ALONE!
THE END

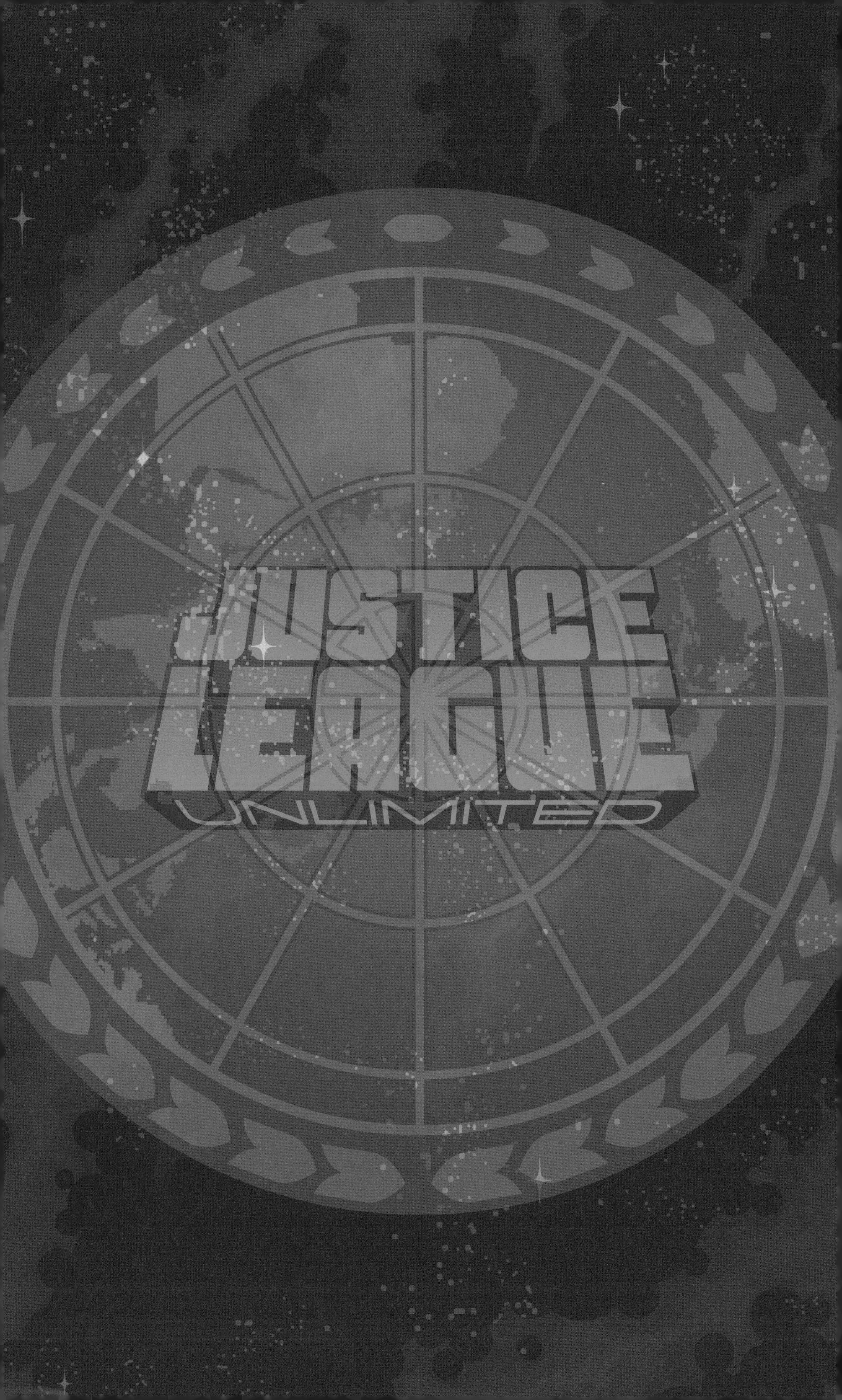
JUSTICE LEAGUE
UNLIMITED

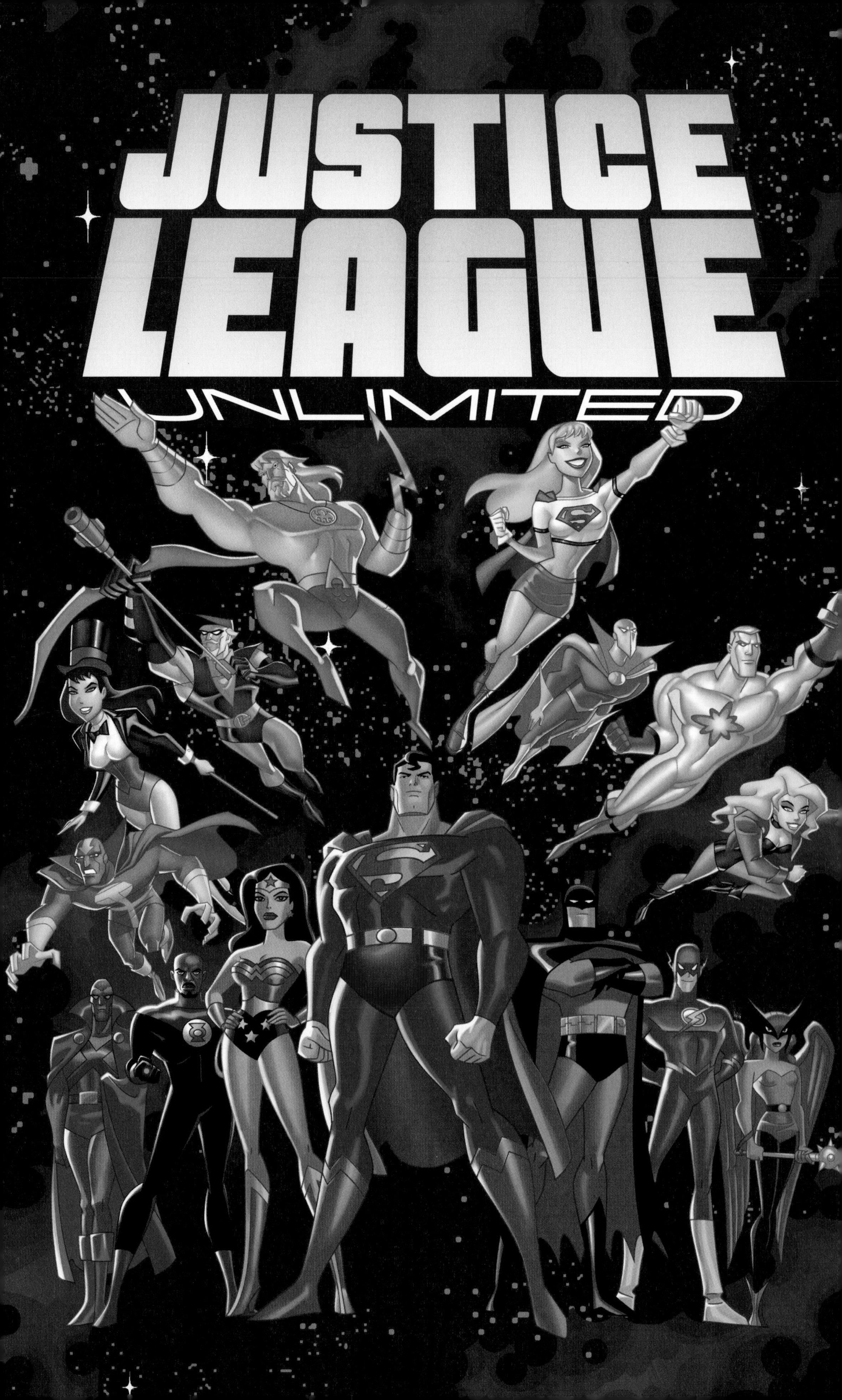
JUSTICE LEAGUE
UNLIMITED

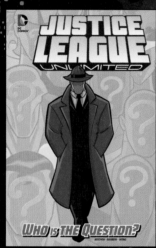

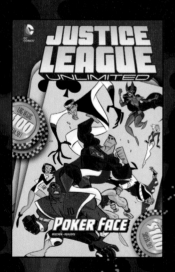

CREATORS

ADAM BEECHEN WRITER

Adam Beechen has written a variety of TV cartoons, including *Ben Ten: Alien Force, Teen Titans, Batman: The Brave and the Bold, The Batman* [for which he received an Emmy nomination], *Rugrats, The Wild Thornberrys, X-Men: Evolution,* and *Static Shock*, as well as the live-action series *Ned's Declassified School Survival Guide* and *The Famous Jett Jackson*. He is also the author of *Hench*, a graphic novel, and has scripted many comic books, including *Batgirl, Teen Titans, Robin,* and *Justice League Unlimited*. In addition Adam has written dozens of children's books, as well as an original young adult novel, *What I Did On My Hypergalactic Interstellar Summer Vacation*.

CARLO BARBERI ARTIST

Carlo Barberi is a professional comic book artist from Monterrey, Mexico. His best-known works for DC Comics include *Batman: The Brave and the Bold*, *The Flash*, *Blue Beetle*, *Gen 13*, and *Justice League Unlimited*.

WALDEN WONG ARTIST

Walden Wong is a professional comic book artist, inker, and colorist. He's worked on some of DC Comics' top characters, including Superman, Batman, Wonder Woman, and more.

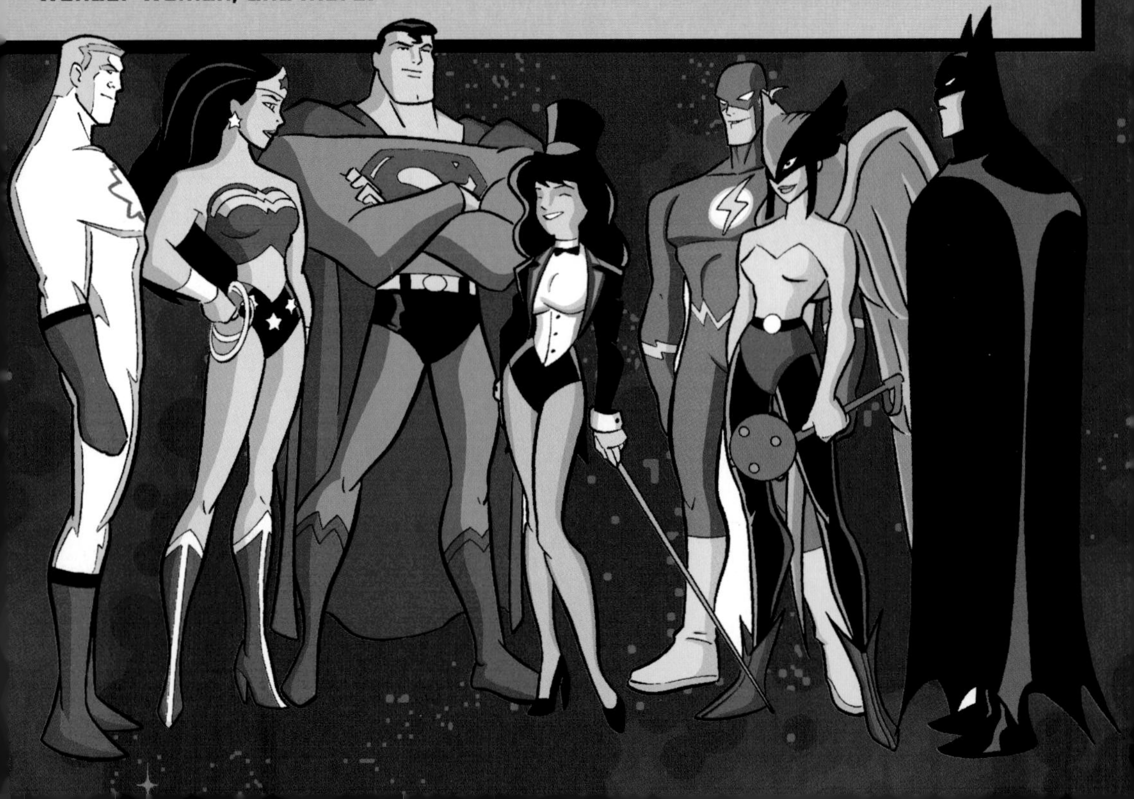

WORD GLOSSARY

distress (diss-TRESS)--in need of help

environmentalist (en-vye-ruh-MEN-tuh-lisst)--any person who advocates or works to protect the air, water, animals, plants, and other natural resources

indestructible (in-di-STRUHK-tuh-buhl)--cannot be destroyed

jarhead (JAHR-hed)--a nickname for a U.S. Marine

overload (oh-vur-LODE)--to send too much energy through a circuit or device that burns it out

quiver (KWIV-ur)--a case or container for arrows

regiment (REJ-uh-ment)--a military unit made up of two or more battalions

seizure (SEE-zhur)--a sudden attack of illness, or a spasm

sensory (SEN-sur-ee)--dealing with the human senses

J.L.U. GLOSSARY

SCREAMER ARROW

One of Green Arrow's special projectiles. These arrows emit deafening sound and blinding light in order to distract and stun targets.

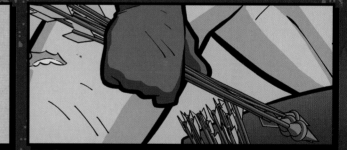

SUPER-SPEED

Like many super heroes, Blue Beetle is capable of moving at superhuman speed.

OW. OW. OW. OW. OW. OW. OW.
BAP
BAP
BAP
BAP

POWER RING

Green Lantern's power ring enables him to create light constructs that move and function just like their real, physical counterparts.

VISUAL QUESTIONS & PROMPTS

1. Green Lantern uses his power ring to capture and control the General. What are some other objects he could have made, or methods he could have used, to capture the General?

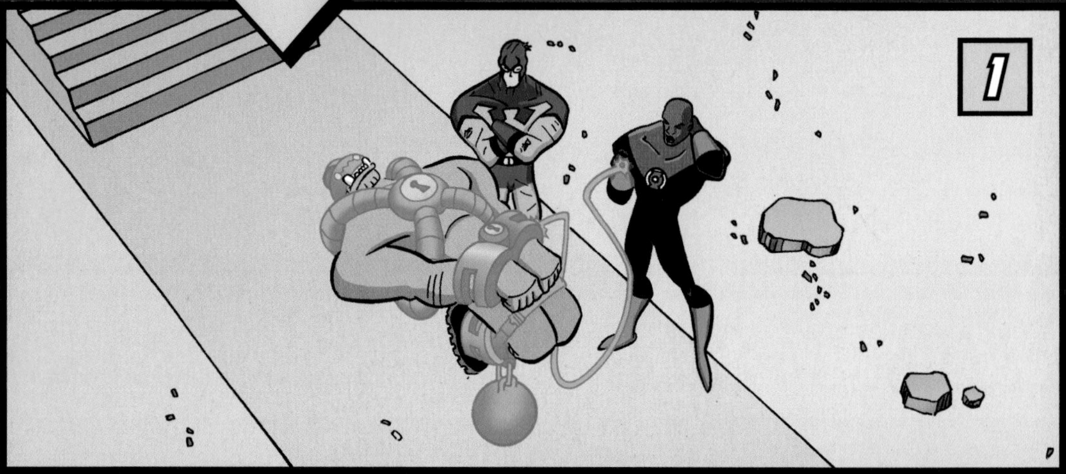

2. Why does this panel have lines passing through it? Read the panels surrounding this one [page 10] for clues.

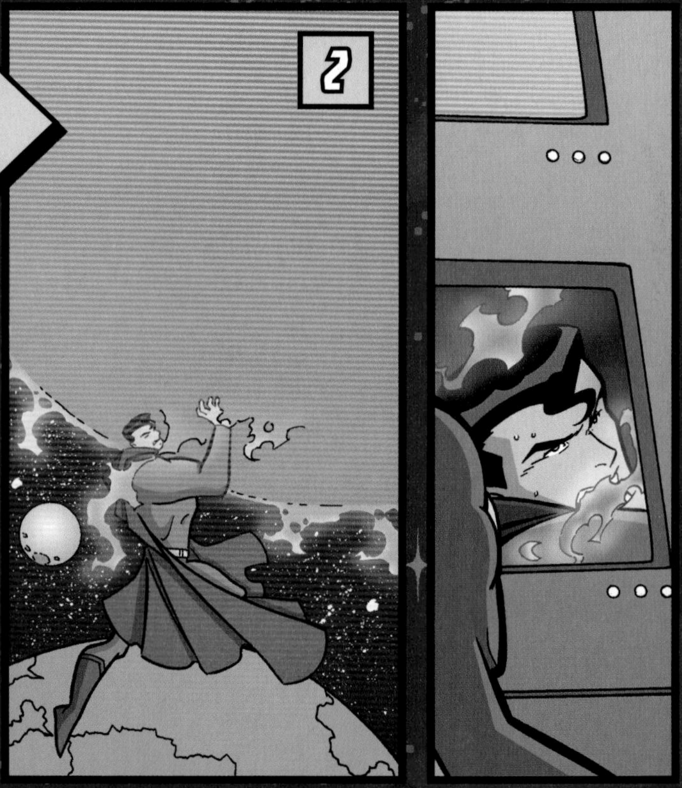

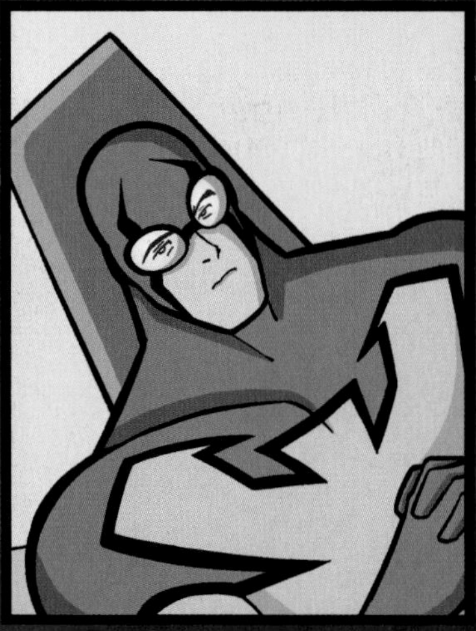

3. In this panel, multiple images of Blue Beetle are shown. Why?

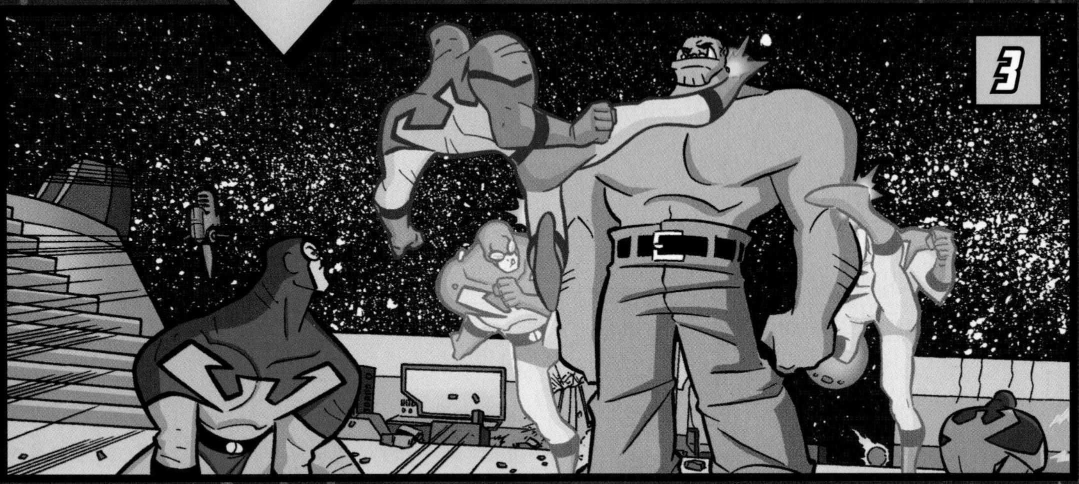
3

4. This panel shows Blue Beetle dressing up in Flash's costume. Why is he doing this? Read the surrounding panels on page 8 for clues.

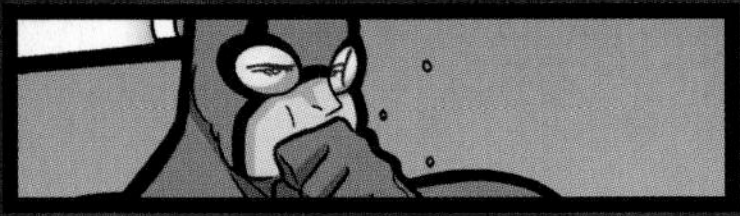

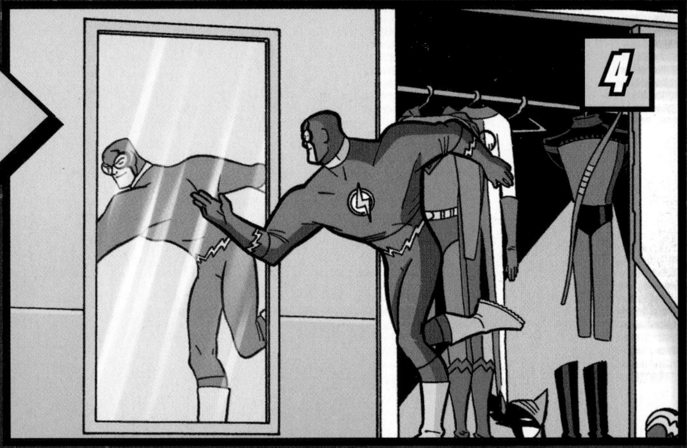
4

5. The background of this panel has a color change, and there are lines heading out from the General's head. Why did the creators choose to do this?

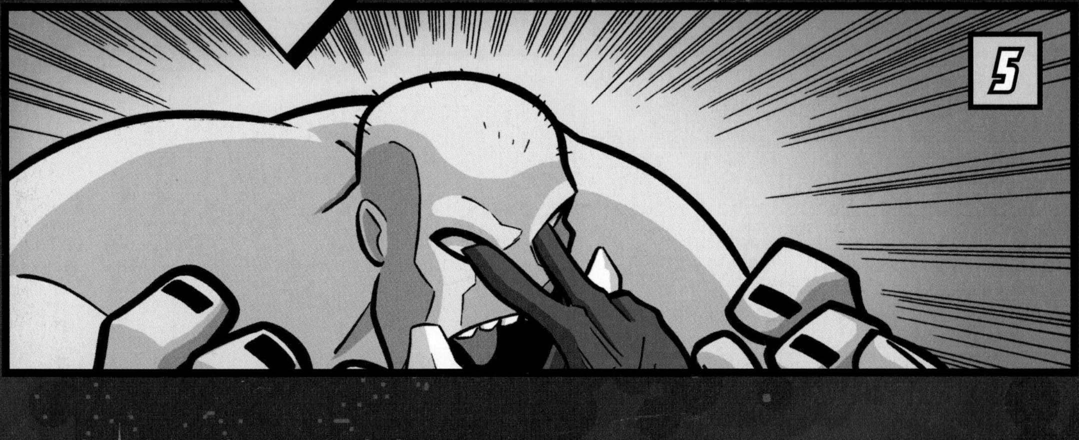
5

WANT EVEN MORE?

GO TO...

www.CAPSTONEKIDS.com

Then find cool websites and more books
like this one at *www.facthound.com*.

Just type in the BOOK ID:
9781434260413